DEATH OF AN ANCIENT SAXON

Doctor Harry Manson, Scotland Yard's Forensic Scientist, was packed off by the Assistant Commissioner (Crime) to a rural country house to recover his health. When Manson opened a book in the library for the sake of a few moments' relaxed reading, it also opened his legendary suspicious mind and led him on to plot and counter-plot, forgery, blackmail — and murder.

E. & M. A. RADFORD

DEATH OF AN ANCIENT SAXON

Complete and Unabridged

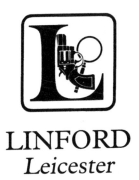

LINFORD
Leicester

First published in Great Britain in 1969 by
Robert Hale Limited, London

First Linford Edition
published 2001
by arrangement with
Robert Hale Limited, London

British Library CIP Data

Radford, Edwin, *1891 – 1973*
 Death of an ancient Saxon.—Large print ed.—
Linford mystery library
 1. Manson, Doctor (Fictitious character)—Fiction
 2. Police—England—London—Fiction
 3. Detective and mystery stories
 4. Large type books
 I. Title II. Radford, M. A. (Mona Augusta)
823.9′14 [F]

ISBN 0–7089–9746–5

Published by
F. A. Thorpe (Publishing)
Anstey, Leicestershire

Set by Words & Graphics Ltd.
Anstey, Leicestershire
Printed and bound in Great Britain by
T. J. International Ltd., Padstow, Cornwall

This book is printed on acid-free paper

1

Doctor Clerebold Forrestal trudged up the roadway — little more than a rural track — that climbed the South Downs in Sussex from the village of Cissing. He walked slowly, pausing now and then to allay his panting. 'Getting too old,' he said to himself. 'That's what's the matter with me. Too old . . . Have to retire . . . can't do the job . . . with this National Health nonsense . . . Retire . . . fifty years gone . . . for nothing . . . hoped . . . one day . . . '

It was not often that he looked back along that avenue of years that had started when as a young, ambitious medico he had planned to start in Sussex a medical dynasty that his hoped-for son and his son's son would carry on into the third and fourth generations after he had himself passed. The dream had been centred in the big house just below the brow of the slope up which he was now climbing.

Eadwin Burstall had lived in that house then, as he did now. For nearly thirty years Burstall had kept his daughter, his only child, chained to his side with the tethers of filial duty — which are stronger than steel, and more durable. When Edgyth — the name is Saxon for 'rich, happy' — had at last rebelled against her chains, seeking the happiness that belonged to her name, and had married her doctor, she died within eighteen months giving birth to the still-born boy whose destined inheritance had been to found the doctor's dynasty.

Forrestal had never married again. Edgyth had been his only love over all the years; he had never forgiven Eadwin Burstall for the years that the locusts had eaten. It was to him that he was now climbing the steep side of the Downs.

He reached the plateau at last. The big house lay ahead looking from its pinnacle at the heights above and the valley below. With his back to it, Forrestal stared round. It was a sight worth seeing, and never failed to move him, though it had been his vision for more than sixty years.

On one side Chanctonbury Ring kept guard from its seven hundred feet over the stretches of the rivers Adur and Arun, its two hundred years' old topnot of beeches hiding its pinnacle. One thousand nine hundred years ago a Roman-Christian temple stood on their site: and worshippers still trudged there three hundred years later. Then it died, and Charles Goring in the 18th Century planted the copse of beeches above its vanished ruins. He lived to such a ripe old age that he saw his saplings grow into trees.

Turning opposite, Forrestal looked in mental vision at Sussex history: at Cissbury Ring, towering with its green sward over every other height on the Sussex Downs. Nearly a thousand and five hundred years back Aella, the Saxon, landed with his sons, Cymen, Whencing and Cissa on the coast near Selsey, and ravaged the Downs, holding them in thrall until his death. His son, Cissa, held the heights after him which became known as Cissing; and also built a stronghold called Cissa's Ceaster, which name today has been demoralised into Chichester; but is still a military stronghold. Aella's second son, Whencing, gave his name to Lancing, on the river's edge below the same Downs.

Forrestal shook himself, and came back to the present. He entered the house. Aelthea Whiting awaited him behind the front door. Aelthea was the niece of old Burstall. Forrestal looked at her, and sighed. She, too, was chained with the tethers of duty as his Edgyth had been he thought, but she would, he knew, hold on to that duty. He nodded to her, inquiry in his glance.

'In the library, doctor,' she analysed the unspoken question. 'He really is ill. I sent for you without telling him, so make it look as though you had dropped in as a friend. The doctor nodded, stepped across the hall and opened a door. 'Good morning, Eadwin,' he greeted. 'Thought you'd have been outside on a nice morning like this.'

'Mornin' Forrestal.' Burstall eyed the bag in the doctor's right hand. "Nother damned fool havin' a baby?' he snapped.

Forrestal smiled.

'Not today, Eadwin. Next Thursday at the earliest. Young woman of one of your farm workers. Just calling on her. Thought I'd look in and see you on the way.'

'No need to lie about it, Forrestal. I ain't deaf and the telephone's in the hall. Aelthea sent for you. Well, now you're here you may as well earn your money. I *am* queer. Been like it for a coupla weeks.'

Doctor Forrestal passed over his little deception. 'Then you should have sent for me before,' he remonstrated. 'Damnit, man, you're 85.' His eyes searched the man. Burstall sat in a deep armchair, his knees wrapped round with a rug though the morning was warm. His face was grey and had a pinched appearance. Forrestal talked as he felt the pulse.

'What's the sleeping like?' he asked.

'Don't sleep at all.'

'Eating?'

'Eat nothing to speak of. Never did.'

'Feel tired?'

'I'm always tired.'

The doctor replaced his watch in his pocket and released the wrist. He produced a roll from his bag. 'Take off your coat,' he ordered, and roll up your left sleeve.' For five minutes he checked by his watch the pressure of blood flowing through the veins of the older man. Then he re-rolled the bandage and packed it away. He stood up.

'Too much whisky, Eadwin,' he said, pointing to the decanter on a table near the man's right hand. 'That's what's the matter with you. Leave the stuff alone. You're an old man and it's getting you down. What's this I hear about your nephew being around again? Thought you'd turned him out and disowned him. How do you expect to feel at your age if you spend half the night with him drowning your inside and your nerves with whisky? You ought to be in bed by nine o'clock. I am when I get the chance. Worst companion you could have is William Rawson.'

'Leave my nephew alone, damn you. It's my say whether he comes here or not. If you want to know, he comes because he's doin' me a bit of good in a business way.'

'Business!' Forrestal chuckled sardonically. 'Thinking of taking your money with you, Eadwin? I should have thought you had more than enough to last the few years left to you. Why the devil do you want to make more? But there, you never did think of anything but money, did you?'

'What's the matter with me?'

'Old age and debility. Tiredness. Low blood pressure. Too low.' He dropped his voice. 'You'll have to take care of yourself, you know. Keep off the spirits. Take a glass of sherry half-an-hour before meals.'

The old man raised his head unexpectedly, and focussed his eyes on the doctor. His face, as hard as the granite of which his house was built, softened a little to the doctor's astonishment; he had never, he thought to himself, seen any softness in the man — and had never expected to.

'Clerebold,' the old man said — and it was the first time in a span of years that he had used the Christian name. 'Clerebold, it's a long time — your family and mine.'

'It is, indeed, Eadwin.'

And it was! For the families interlocked with the ancient history of Sussex, though time had played shufflecock with their names. The *Atteborstalle* in the Hundred Rolls of 1273 had been an old name centuries earlier, but had now come to Burstall, though the prefix, Eadwin, had remained in its original form; over centuries the eldest son of the house had been christened Eadwin. Too, the history of surnames was bound up with Burstall. A Saxon had one day trudged up the side of the Downs to found a *feorm* and build for himself a *cottsetla*. He was called by the Downs-people 'the man up the winding path', and the Saxon word for that was *Atterborstalle*. By 1200 A.D. it was shortened to Burstall; and Burstall it still was. But the Saxon, *Eadwin*, Borstall still retained with his great frame and the flaxen hair of his race — until age whitened but never thinned it.

A hundred years after *Atteborstalle* another Saxon, Osbert, had rented out space in a paddock for horses. The Saxon name for a farm paddock was *forstalle*.

Osbert became named as Osbert de la Forstalle; and Doctor Clerebold Forrestal was his descendant. Thus a common heritage and family tradition had bound Burstall and Forrestal together since boyhood days.

'It's a long time,' Burstall said again. 'I'm the last direct of my line, Clerebold. No male to carry on the heritage.'

'That's your own fault,' Forrestal said, brutally. 'Had you let Edgyth come to me in our good time, there could have been a son, or two for you through me.'

'Am I going to die, Clerebold?'

'I see no reason why you should not live to be a hundred, Eadwin, if you take care of yourself . . . No, don't get up. I'll let myself out and have a word with Aelthea, and send you a tonic.'

Aelthea Whiting — even in the female line the family had preserved its Saxon heritage — hearing him close the door of the library called to him from the morning-room. She was a shade over thirty years, tall and slender with a cultured voice — the voice of a woman well poised and sure of herself. She was

9

unmarried. Many a man had made the suggestion of an escort to this slender girl whose pleasantly moulded figure and expressional face was surmounted by a halo of golden hair upswept to a crown of curls. One by one they had dropped out of the chase. She had come to the house shortly after her eighteenth birthday when her mother, Eadwin Burstall's only sister, had died, leaving her orphaned daughter a legacy to her brother.

Burstall had cursed at the improvidence of his brother-in-law who had failed to amass sufficent from his toiling to leave his family self-supporting. He had sent a grudging invitation to the girl to stay with him until she found a situation. But, he had hinted, there was a limit to his period of hospitality.

The situation had not developed; old Eadwin quickly discovered that his niece was accomplished in domestic arts. When, from time to time offers of employment had come to her, and had been tentatively mentioned, the old man pointed out that he had given her a good home for a considerable time, and she now owed him a duty in his declining years. It was the same argument he had used to his daughter more than twenty years earlier; the result was the same in both cases; Aelthea, like Edgyth before her, had stayed on as a duty.

She had become more necessary to the old man when, after a violent scene, he had pushed his nephew, William Rawson, to the hall door, held him there with one hand while he got the door open, and had then kicked him through the portal with the parting injunction, 'never darken these doors again.'

Aelthea never learned the reason for the banishment; but it had chained her more securely than ever to the old man, for she was now his only relative. With a cook and a couple of maids, she maintained the house on the breast of the Downs, feeding and keeping warm its irascible master.

It was made clear that she would inherit the old man's money; Burstall had exhibited the new will to her and to Doctor Forrestal before writing on the envelope the name of his solicitors, and dropping it in the postbox at the gate, which the postman cleared each evening.

Nothing was heard of William Rawson for years, until he suddenly appeared again at the house, and apparently on friendly terms with his uncle.

Doctor Forrestal made reference to the return when Aelthea turned from her dusting to meet him. 'What's Rawson doing here, Aelthea?' he asked.

'I don't know, doctor. Business, he says. What *is* the matter with uncle?'

Doctor Forrestal thought for a moment, wrinkling his brows at the same time. 'Can't say, definitely, my dear. Probably a combination of things. He has low blood pressure and I've never known him have that before. His pulse is slow and he is excited, and, of course, he is an old man. But I hadn't expected him to break up so quickly. I'm sending him a tonic. See that he takes it regularly.'

'Is he . . . ?'

'No, no, Aelthea.' The doctor broke into her sentence. 'There is no reason to suppose that Eadwin will die before he wants to. He's looking forward to making more money with the help of Rawson. I should say he's more like to lose some with that scoundrel.'

The tonic seemed to make little difference. Eadwin Burstall experienced daytime rallies followed by evening relapses. From wandering in the garden, the old man took to sitting in the sun lounge, showing little interest in his surroundings, and forgetting even to censure the household accounts, a proceeding for which over the years he had each week demonstrated a parsimonious enthusiasm.

The doctor toiled once more up the long hill and grunted a greeting as he entered the bedroom. But one look at Eadwin Burstall killed the words on his lips. Two or three minutes was sufficient for an examination; he went with unaccustomed agility to the telephone and called a Harley Street specialist. For twenty-four hours Burstall lay weakly protesting at his condition. Movement made him pant noisily; he was unable to rise to a sitting position without help, and his speech was low and husky.

Sir Charles Hurley, who had hurried

from his Harley Street rooms, listened to Doctor Forrestal's history of the case, and then spent half-an-hour with the patient. He gave his verdict.

'There is no disease as far as I can ascertain, Forrestal,' he said. 'The man seems to be just worn out. He's an old man, and I dare say he has lived well?'

'Yes, he was always a high liver. Never had anything radically wrong with him all the time I've known him, and that's well nigh sixty years. Thing that worries me is the short time he seems to have gone to pieces.'

'Often happens, my dear chap. He's been a strong man and full of health up to . . . what age is he?'

'Eighty-five.'

'Well, time has taken its toll. I don't say he'll die yet, but it won't be long.' He outlined a line of treatment and departed on his journey back to London.

Doctor Forrestal outlined the position to William Rawson and Aelthea. 'He should have a nurse, I think,' he said. 'I doubt if I'll be able to get one today, but . . . '

'I'll sit with him till midnight,' Rawson said, 'if Aelthea will take on from then. Then perhaps you can get a nurse tomorrow.'

But a nurse was not necessary. At nine in the morning Eadwin Burstall died. Doctor Forrestal certified his death as due to cardiac failure, due to old age.

2

They buried Eadwin Burstall three days later: Only eight people followed him to his rest: Aelthea Whiting, William Rawson, Doctor Forrestal, and Edward Swinburne, the old man who had been lawyer to the Burstalls for forty years; and four old residents of Cissing who had been Eadwin's cronies in the past years — and hoped against hope that he had remembered them in his will.

Swinburne had spent the previous night with Forrestal. They had talked well into the night. 'Well, he's gone, Forrestal,' the lawyer had said. 'The last of the Saxons!'

'Not quite, my friend,' the doctor contradicted. 'There is still myself. Eadwin was inordinately proud of his descent — and so am I. I doubt if there are fifty families in the country who can trace an unbroken descent to Saxon times, and with their patronymic — he with *Eadwin* and me with *Clerebold*, which was *Clarembald* when the last of the Saxon kings died. There are Norman descents, mebbe, many of them, but not Saxons.'

The mortal remains of Burstall were laid in the family vault. Doctor Forrestal went in with the bearers. Not since he had put his Edgyth to rest had he been inside the marble vault. As the bearers lifted the coffin on to the ledge beside that of Edgyth, Forrestal took from a pocket a little bunch of daisies and placed it on the old coffin that housed all that he had hoped for in life. She had always loved daisies. He touched the wood lingeringly, and then turned aside to hide his tears. A few minutes more and the mourners entered the cars for the return journey leaving Eadwin Burstall alone, with all his money behind him.

Back at the house lunch was eaten in silence. It was after coffee had been served that the company adjourned to the library for the reading of the will. Mr. Swinburne opened his case and from it extracted a number of documents. He spread them out in front of him at the end of the table, perched his old-fashioned spectacles on the end of his nose, cleared his throat, and addressed the family.

'As you will know, the late Mr. Burstall was a warm man,' he began. 'I cannot give the precise figures until I have gone carefully through his affairs, but I expect the estate to realise something over £100,000. My old friend made two wills. The first was some years ago, and was made by himself and sent to me. But exactly seven years ago he requested me to attend on him here bringing the will with me. I did so, and at his request handed the will to him. Also at his request I drew up a second will for him, and that is the document which I am now to read for you.'

Mr. Swinburne lifted up a sealed envelope and opened it. He extracted a document and began to read. ' 'I, Eadwin Burstall, of 'Hengeclif' (even in the name of his house, he stuck to the Saxon — *hengeclif* meant a overhanging edifice) in the county of Sussex, being of sound mind do hereby revoke all other wills . . . ' ' He began the preamble. He droned on for two or three minutes to an inattentive audience until he reached the substance of the will — the bequests. Then he addressed the company.

'I think, perhaps, as the staff are mentioned in the will they should be present to hear the bequests,' he suggested. Aelthea left the room to return within a minute or so with the servants. Mr. Swinburne addressed them. 'You are to hear the dispositions of your late master. All of you are mentioned by the kindness of Mr. Burstall. Listen, please. I give and bequeath to Esther Morrison, if she is still in my service and not under notice, the sum of £250 in recognition of her long service in my household.' Mr. Swinburne looked across at Aelthea. 'This woman, I suppose, is not under notice?' he asked.

'She is not, and she would be the last person I can think of whom I should want to rid myself.'

Esther burst into loud sobbing. 'He was

a good master,' she said, wiping her streaming eyes. 'Not, mind you, as he was easy to work for,' she added energetically.

Mr. Swinburne tapped a pencil on the table. 'To Alice Mentmore if still in my service and not under notice the sum of £200.' He looked again at Aelthea, and received an affirming nod. 'To Daphne Crooks, £20 for each year of service.' Mr. Swinburne put down the document. 'That is all that concerns you,' he said addressing the servants. 'You can now withdraw.'

The door closed behind them, the lawyer continued. 'To my nephew, William Rawson, I give and bequeath as a duty the sum of £500.'

'Most kind of uncle, I must say. Family ties must have been a strong point with him.'

'To my old friend and son-in-law Clerebold Forrestal I leave £5,000 and any momento of me he may care to choose. The residue of my estate I give and bequeath absolutely to my niece, Aelthea Whiting.'

Mr. Swinburne put down the will,

removed his glasses and glanced at the girl. 'I must congratulate you on your inheritance,' he said, primly. 'It comes as no surprise of course, but I should tell you that my late client expressed to me his feelings of the sacrifices you made in staying with him, and he was very appreciative of the way in which you ran this house — especially in the economic way,' he added, a little dryly.

He returned to the will. 'There are one or two details to be taken note of. For instance, this house and its contents are particularly mentioned as the inheritance of Miss Whiting, and there is a provision that the house shall be maintained as a residence and not sold or left vacant. This, I may say, was a very firmly expressed view of my late client. It appeared also in the earlier will of which I spoke.'

William Rawson looked up. A quizzical smile played round his lips. 'Did that earlier will give me the residue of the estate?' he asked.

'You have no right to put that question and it should not have been put,' the lawyer said, sternly. 'But since you *have* asked it I will reply. That will left the residue of the estate in equal sums between you and Miss Whiting.'

The uncomfortable pause which followed was broken by the lawyer addressing Aelthea. 'I should like, Miss Whiting, to go through my late client's papers in order to be in a position to prepare the estate for probate. And I should like, of course, your authority to continue to act for the estate.'

'That goes without saying, Mr. Swinburne. All uncle's papers were kept in his desk.' She indicated a large roll-top desk of ancient pattern in front of a large sidebay window. Shall we leave you here?'

She served tea to her cousin and Doctor Forrestal. Rawson was the first to refer to the matter of the two wills. 'I ought to have congratulated you before, Aelthea,' he said, pleasantly, 'but I do so now. There's no malice from me. I asked Swinburne if the earlier will had left me property because I rather wanted to know how much my quarrel with uncle had cost. Well, I know now. I don't need the money, I've sufficient to have a good time on, and I am quite sure you will make better use of the estate than I would have done. For one thing I certainly wouldn't have lived in the place. I'd have gone mad. The village is worse than the house.'

'That is very nice of you, William.' Aelthea was pleasantly surprised at the manner in which Rawson had heard of his disinheritance; she had expected some recriminations when they were left together. 'You are welcome to stay here whenever you like. I will have a suite always ready for you.'

'That's kind of you.' He rose. 'Now, I'll have to be getting back to London. I've lost a lot of time from business lately, and . . .'

Before he could complete the sentence the door of the room opened so violently that it swung on its hinges and cracked against the stopper. Mr. Swinburne came through the opening clutching a document in his fingers. He walked unsteadily, jerkily and after a surprised glance Doctor Forrestal rose quickly to his feet and stepped to his side.

'What is the matter, Mr. Swinburne? Are you ill?' he asked sharply, for the lawyer's face was white and drawn and his hands were trembling. He presented the appearance of a man suddenly overwhelmed by some enormous shock. He sank into a chair and mopped his brow with a handkerchief.

'A dreadful thing,' he said in a voice hardly above a whisper. 'Incredible . . . incomprehensible . . . I have never had such a thing happen to me.'

'What is reprehensible, Swinburne?' asked Rawson.

Swinburne turned away from the nephew and looked across at Aelthea Whiting. 'Dreadful news my dear lady . . . reprehensible,' he repeated again. 'I have found a new will.'

A stunned silence followed the announcement. Rawson was the first to break it. 'A new will, did you say. Extradordinary.'

'The point is, Swinburne, what difference does it make, if any, to the disposition of the estate?' Forrestal asked.

'It makes a marked difference,' the

lawyer said. 'Under it — and it is duly attested and witnessed — though the bequests to Doctor Forrestal and the staff are confirmed, the estate is left — I am quoting the wording — 'to my nephew, William Rawson' after an earlier provision of £5,000 to Miss Whiting.'

A startled exclamation came from Rawson. 'To me? Why?'

'As to that there is no intimation, sir.'

'When was this document executed?' the doctor asked.

'Apparently on January the tenth, just four months ago.'

'That was before I returned here,' said Rawson. There was a note of surprise in his voice.

'The document is signed and witnessed?' Doctor Forrestal asked. The lawyer nodded. 'The witnesses are Isaac Jones and Israel Cooper. Who are they?'

'Jones is the gardener and odd job man,' explained Aelthea.

'And Cooper?'

'Was the afternoon postman. But he was buried a month ago.'

'Are you sure the document is genuine,'

Forrestal demanded.

'So far as I can see, yes. It appears to be in the handwriting of Burstall which is well known to me. You, also, doctor should know it.' He passed the document over.

Doctor Forrestal adjusted his glasses and stared at the double sheet of paper. He read it carefully, line by line, to the signature at the end. Then he nodded and handed it back. 'It's Eadwin's writing. The 'S's' and the 't's' are what I looked for. I have never known any other person make them like Eadwin did.'

'My uncle appears to have made a habit of drawing up wills,' Rawson said. 'Where did you come across this one, may I ask?'

'Among the papers in Mr. Burstall's desk. Its envelope was marked 'to be opened after my death'. It was sealed and included a bunch of documents relating to stocks.' Mr. Swinburne mopped his brow. 'My first thought was that it was the old will which had been nullified by the one I read out to you just now. Then I saw the date.'

'Apart from the date is this new will a copy of the older one, the earlier document?' Forrestal asked.

'No, sir, it is not. There is a difference of some £2,000 in the bequest to Miss Whiting,' said Swinburne. 'You say — he looked at the girl — that the second of the two witnesses is dead. Is it possible for me to interview the other witness — the gardener, I think you said.'

Aelthea nodded, and left the room, to return a few minutes later with Isaac Jones. Mr. Swinburne produced a fountain pen and a sheet of paper and passed them to him. 'Sit down here, my man, and sign your name on this piece of paper. Write as you always do when you sign a letter.' Laboriously, Jones scrawled out his name. Mr. Swinburne took it and compared it with the signature on the will. He nodded, passed it to Miss Whiting and to Doctor Forrestal. 'As far as I can see, and making allowances for the fact that an uneducated person rarely writes his name in the same way twice, it seems to me to be a replica of the signature on this document,' he announced. He turned again to Jones. 'Did you, my man, recently sign any paper for your master?' he asked. 'I want you to think carefully, because it is most important.'

'Sign papers, sir?' The man looked up in surprise. 'I was allus signin' papers for the master. He said as'ow I wuz his legal witness.'

'When did you sign the last one, Jones?'

'It maum be about six weeks gone.'

'Would it have been, or did you sign something, three months ago?'

'I wouldn't like to be sure certain. All I know is as I wuz allus signin' papers.'

'You knew Israel Cooper, did you?'

'I wur one as carried him to his grave, sir.'

To a townsman, the answer might appear to be evasive, but not to a rural countryman. For in these rural areas of Britain only those who had been the closest friends of the dead man would carry out their last service as bearers of his coffin at the funeral.

'Did Israel ever tell you he had signed a paper for the master?'

Doctor Forrestal asked the question. He was more likely to get a true answer than a stranger.

'No, doctor, he never said anything to me.'

'Was his name on this paper when you signed?'

'No, doctor. There was nothing on it save me name.'

'All right. You may go now. And keep your mouth shut, my man,' the lawyer said. When the door had closed: 'Well, that seems to settle the matter. He remembers signing a document, and here is his signature on the will. I feel bound to say, with all respect to Mr. Rawson, that I consider the terms of this will most unfair to Miss Whiting. As I said before, Burstall has always spoken to me of the high regard in which he held his niece. I look upon this will with great disfavour and I shall prove it with reluctance.' He mopped his brow at the end of this rather one-sided oration, and regarded Rawson with some misgiving.

'I entirely agree with you,' Rawson said, unexpectedly. 'I think cousin Aelthea has been very badly treated. I do not intend to accept its provisions entirely so far as she is concerned. I shall pay from the estate the amount which was given her in the earlier will of which Mr. Swinburne has spoken.

'As for the provision that this house shall be maintained as a residence and not sold or left vacant, I have no intention of living in the place. Aelthea can live here with pleasure; if she doesn't, I shall let it furnished. There is nothing against that in the will, is there Mr. Swinburne?'

'No, I don't think there can be any objection to that,' the lawyer said. 'I must point out, of course, that Miss Whiting has the right to contest the will . . . in view of the great difference in the bequests. It might be possible to prove that the bequests are such as Mr. Burstall had no intention of making, judging by his remarks to me and other people, and the fact that they are in the document might be due to the fact that he was not in a fit state to execute a will; in other words the Courts might hold that, in view of his often expressed sentiments and intentions, this will was not that of a man of sound mind. There is also the fact, which seems to have been proved by the gardener, that the witnesses to the document did not sign, as the law requires, in the presence of the testator and *each other* . . .'

Aelthea Whiting interrupted. 'There is to be no question of any such proceeding, Mr. Swinburne.' There was determination in her voice, softly though she spoke. 'I do not profess to understand the reason for this strange, this very strange revulsion of feeling against me by my uncle, but that is apparently what he wanted to do, and he did it. I shall not contest his wishes in any way.' She turned to Rawson. 'It is now my turn to congratulate you, cousin William in the same generous way that you gave your best wishes to me. And I thank you for your generous offer to increase the amount mentioned in the will. That is the sum Uncle wanted to give me from his estate, and that is the sum I shall take. That, and no more. I shall, of course, leave here as soon as I can find other accommodation . . .'

'But why, cousin Aelthea,' Rawson burst out. 'That is the last thing I want. I would like you to remain and take care of the place. And it has been your home for years. Why cannot you stay here?'

'That is very good of you, cousin William, but I prefer to cut clean away from the old surroundings, which could only be very painful to me.'

Mr. Swinburne rose. 'Then I take it I can go ahead with proving the will?' he asked. 'I will do so as soon as I have been able to ascertain the value of the estate. In the meantime, Mr. Rawson, you can, of course, draw on me for any money you may require; and Miss Whiting will, of course, look to you for the expenses of running this establishment.'

'If you are returning to London, Mr. Swinburne, I should like to accompany you,' Rawson said. 'I have to get back to business at least for a few days.' The two men left the room together.

Aelthea and the doctor were left alone amid the debris of the dramatically interrupted tea. For some minutes they remained silent; a sense of restraint made itself conscious between them: the restraint that inevitably comes between friends in a moment of sympathy or concern. It was Aelthea who broke the silence. 'There is nothing to be said, is there, doctor?' she asked: she had read his thoughts pretty well. Forrestal brought his eyes to meet hers. There was, he saw, a quiet smile on the girl's face. But he noted — being a doctor — it did not reach her lips. He had seen that smile so often on the faces of people who had been hurt, or were fighting for what he knew — and they knew — to be inevitable. It is the fixed smile of courage; no smile is genuine that does not sparkle in the eyes and show in parted lips; it is either a resigned smile, or a cruel one. He made answer.

'It is to my mind a wicked will, Aelthea,' he said. 'But I am afraid it is in keeping with Eadwin. He was a very wicked and cruel man. He always had a selfish streak in him.'

She looked at her companion. 'I have sometimes thought you had no great love for him, Doctor. I always had the impression that he had done you some wrong, yet, at the funeral . . . ' She paused in confusion.

'The tears were not for him,' Forrestal replied, quietly. 'He did me a great wrong once. He probably did not regard it as a wrong; I think he looked upon it as his right.' Gently, Forrestal told the girl of his Edgyth, of his dream, and the dying of it. 'I wondered sometimes, whether you were destined to go the same way,' he said.

'It might well have been so, doctor. But the destiny has been broken. I should not have stayed here so long, but for his claim that I was essential for his comfort. I am afraid that I should not have stayed had he lived much longer. And now . . . '

'That sounds as though you do not intend to stay here much longer.'

She nodded her head in assent. 'I shall leave within the next few days. I shall recommend to William that Esther Morrison be made housekeeper. She will be a good one, I think. And with nobody here she and the two maids can keep the place aired and tidy.'

'Have you any plans for the future?'

The girl nodded. 'I shall' — she hesitated for a moment or two, and then added — 'be married.'

'Married?' Doctor Forrestal looked up startled. 'I had no idea you were that way inclined.'

'Because I have not gone out with any man locally, doctor? It is not anyone near here. I met him on holiday in Devonshire. Marriage was impossible since I could not leave here, but now that uncle is dead there is no barrier. Gerald hasn't much money, and life for me will be very different from this — ' she indicated with a wave of a hand the house and garden. 'But I think I shall be content. Uncle gave me more than he thought when he died. I might have met the same fate that befell your love.'

Doctor Forrestal looked away. 'I suppose you haven't any idea what could have induced Eadwin to make a new will? He hadn't shown any sign of animosity?'

'Not the least idea. On the contrary, he seemed towards the end to go out of his way to say kind things to me. I think he knew he was not going to live much longer, and seemed grateful to me for my attention. That is why I cannot understand this new will.'

'He was a wicked man, my dear,' said Forrestal, and took his leave.

A week later Aelthea left 'Hengeclif'. Rawson endeavoured to keep her. 'I would rather go, cousin,' she insisted. 'But I would like to leave the greater part of my things here until I have somewhere to house them,' she asked.

'Keep them here as long as you like, and come and spend a holiday whenever you like. I am going abroad for some time and, in view of my inheritance, am giving up business. I shall probably decide to live abroad.' They shook hands and parted. Three months later she found that Rawson had paid £2,000 into her banking account with the instruction that it was not to be notified to her until a certain specified date.

3

Commander Harry Manson, barrister-at-law, slowly dressed himself. He put on his shirt. He pulled over his front stud the snowy-white stiff collar, and tied round it a neat, grey-stippled bow tie. He pulled on his waistcoat and slipped a jacket over it. The general ensemble inspected in a mirror, he sat down in a chair and spoke to a man writing at a desk.

'Well, Sir Charles?' he asked.

The *mise en scene* was the Harley Street consulting room of Sir Charles Hurley, consultant to Scotland Yard and the Home Office. His patient, Harry Manson, Doctor of Science, and Barrister-at-law, was a Commander of Scotland Yard C.I.D. He was also head of the Forensic Laboratory and of the Homicide branch.

'Well, Sir Charles?' he asked again.

The specialist finished entering notes on an index card. Then, he laid his pen aside, rose, and stood straddling the empty fireplace, an athletic figure in striped trousers, lavender waistcoat and flowing black cravat tie, and black coat.

Looking at the detective he marked the high forehead, the deepset eyes and the aesthetic face that are the mark of the scholar. He noted, too, the slight stoop of the shoulders which is also the invariable mark of the scholar, though why a scholar should have to bear this misfortune has never been properly explained. Sir Charles noted these; and he marked, also, the drawn lines in the face, the wrinkles at the corners of the eyes, and the furrows on the high forehead. These, he knew, came only when Doctor Manson was worried in his duties as Scotland Yard's scientific adviser and investigator. They came and they went, as his investigations bore fruit, but lately they had been there continually.

Doctor Manson had himself recognised the signs. Since he had forsaken his role as an amateur criminologist and acceded to the persuasions of Sir Edward Allen, the Assistant Commissioner (C) to found a scientific laboratory at the Yard and control it, he had borne the responsibility of a score or more major crimes for aid in solving which the Yard's assistance had been asked.

Without respite he had applied himself to microscope, chemicals and reagents, and his clear and rapier-like brain had sought for, and found, clues and had followed them to their inevitable end — the unearthing of the criminal who, when he is pitted against modern science can have no chance of escape, always supposing that modern forensic science is properly applied.

But Doctor Manson had found the task getting beyond him. The logical reasoning which had always been a *tour de force* in his investigations, had more than once in recent weeks led him into paths of error. His conclusions after experiments had been arrived at only after considerable doubt and hesitation completely foreign to his collated brain.

Sir Edward Allen, noticing the strain and concerned over it, had sent him to Sir Charles Hurley. 'It is of no use to flog a willing horse, Harry,' he had said: and Manson realising the wisdom of the advice had made an appointment with the specialist. Sir Charles had probed with the same intensity of concentration and energy that his patient was wont to use in another avenue of science. At the end Manson had put his query, 'Well, Sir Charles?'

The specialist dangled his pince-nez on its silken cord. 'There is nothing wrong with you bodily, Doctor,' he said. 'You are as sound, physically as a man only two-thirds your age. Why, I do not know. You take no exercise beyond an occasional fishing trip. You spend your time leaning over a bench. Yet you are as fine an animal as ever I have examined.

'But your brain is tired. You are living on your nerves. While that can fortify you for a time, it cannot go on for ever. The driving of the nerves leads, inevitably, to a neurotic state. That effects the tissues of the brain, and in its turn results in the decay of the intellect. You have reached the first stage.

'Go away from Scotland Yard. Forget

crime and criminals. Don't look into a microscope. Go right into the country and stay there. You have the summer in front of you. Keep in the open air. Play golf, if you haven't forgotten how to play; and if you have forgotten, start to learn it all over again.' He paused, and searched round in a drawer of his desk. 'Upon my soul, I believe I have the very place for you. He read out from a paper:

TO LET, FURNISHED: Country house in picturesque position on the South Downs at Cissing, Sussex. Golf, fishing, riding. Housekeeper and maids on the premises. Three months or longer if desired.

'Ideal, Manson. Do you know the country?' he asked. Doctor Manson shook his head.

'Well, I do. And I know the house. Had a patient there quite recently. I should say it is just the place for you and Alice. Take a rod with you as you are fond of fishing. There is a library of books for you to go at in the evenings, and the four winds of

41

heaven as your neighbours. And three months is just about the period I would prescribe for you.'

Doctor Manson drove down to Cissing next day. A fortnight later he was installed in 'Hengeclif.'

'I'll drop a note to Clerebold Forrestal,' Sir Charles told him as the scientist paid him a final visit. 'He's the only doctor in the place. Getting on in years, but a sound man who has wasted his life in the district. He'll look after you and see you keep to the rules. And now, don't let me see you again for three months.'

For a fortnight Doctor Manson, looked after by his wife and the housekeeper, walked and slept. From the moment that he stood on the lawn and viewed the prospect of the Downs, of Cissbury Ring and Chanctonbury, he knew that Sir Charles had been right when he said that the spot was an ideal one for him. He and Alice — she was the daughter and heiress of the millionaire financier, Charles Wendover — walked without ceasing — to Chanctonbury, where they wandered among the prehistoric entrenchment beneath the crown of beeches; to the double rampart and ditches of the early Iron Age fortress that is now Cissbury Ring; on to the heights of Ditchling Beacon. They rode at a fast canter over the gallops that belong to Ryan Price, the trainer at Findon; and essayed a leisurely game of golf on the municipal links at Worthing.

The evenings were spent in the library. Esther laid a fire for the air was still a little chilly, and Doctor Manson ensconsed in front of it in an armchair and with coffee or whisky-and-soda by his side, dipped into a book taken at random from the shelves.

The Doctor, taking a cursory glance at the bookshelves on the occasion of his first visit of exploration to Cissing had been more than a little surprised at the extent and catholicity of the library. Cheek by jowl stood classical editions so diverse as the English translation of Zeno's *Socrates*, and Shaw's *Essays in Fabian Socialism*; Cranmer-Byng's *Chinese Feast of Lanterns*, and Clark's

Mesolithic Settlement of Northern Europe. The many hundred volumes ran the gamut of prehistoric antiquities, art from Greek to Futurism, history, biography, drama and mathematics. Literature accounted for scores of volumes, from philosophy to the modern novel; from Lucretius to James Agate.

The late owner of 'Hengeclif', Doctor Manson ruminated, had a scholar's library, yet he found no evidence that the man himself was a scholar. He made a mental note to ask Doctor Forrestal, when he saw him, whether the owner had indeed collected the books of so wide a range, or whether, as he really thought, the library had been purchased for the purpose of lining the room and converting a room into a country mansion library.

Doctor Forrestal made his visit on the sixteenth day of Manson's stay. He had decided to let the patient settle down before he called on him for the purpose of comparing his condition with the résumé explained in Sir Charles Hurley's letter. 'There is no sense in analysing soda water while it's still fizzing,' he had said to himself.

He found the scientist not exactly fizzing, but decidedly not as flat as soda water which had ceased to effervesce. 'I feel a better man already,' Manson told him after they had greeted each other.

Forrestal smiled the charming smile that had made him popular in Cissing over the years. 'So I should imagine, seeing you after having read Sir Charles's letter to me. Sleeping well?'

'Like a log.'

'Taking the air?'

'Walking as I haven't walked for years.'

'Fond of fishing, Doctor?'

'It's my one hobby. Salmon, mostly — and trout.'

'Well, we can't give you that here. But there's good coarse fishing in the rivers, and there's quite a bit of private water I can get you into.'

It was after lunch, as they sat with coffee, that Doctor Manson inquired after the library's books.

'Yes, Eadwin was a knowledgeable man,' Forrestal replied. 'But he had nothing special in the way of education. A good tutor, I think.'

'But these . . . ' Manson waved a hand at the shelves. 'Did he buy them and read them? If he did . . . '

'I don't think Eadwin bought them to read. His father was something of a learned man, and the books *came* to him. All except his special corner . . . Here.'

He crossed with the doctor to a shelf near the window. Manson eyed the titles. 'H'm! *Beowulf* by Clark Hall, Skeats's *Anglo-Saxon Gospels*, and what's this? *Cartularium Saxonicum*, and an Anglo-Saxon Grammar — Siever's, I see, with Clark Hall's A.S. dictionary. Took an interest in the Anglo-Saxon period, eh?'

Forrestal chuckled. 'He lived in it, Doctor. It was life to him. Come to that, so do I. You see we are among the very few who claim direct descent from those times. I'm not sure that we are not the only ones left — or at least I am.' He told the Doctor of the old man's pride in his race and his sorrow at the fact that he had no son to carry on the family.

'Sad, that,' Manson said. 'They tell me

he's abroad now.'

'Who? Eadwin? I don't know where he is, but I've a pretty good idea,' he said with a chuckle. 'He's dead.'

'Dead! The solicitors told me he was living in the South of France.'

'The owner? Oh, that's William Rawson, old Eadwin's nephew. He isn't the man who collected the books. He's an outsider — his father wasn't Saxon, you see. Only book he ever reads is Ruff's *Guide to the Turf.*'

'Queer.' Doctor Manson looked up with sudden interest.

'Oh, not *that* kind of queer,' retorted Forrestal. 'There's nothing in it in your line. But it's an odd story.'

'If it's an odd story, Forrestal, I'd like to hear it. I'm very fond of odd stories.'

Doctor Forrestal settled down in his chair. Manson poured out a couple of whiskies and soda and settled down with him. Step by step the old doctor took him through the story of the two wills, the disinheritance, first of the nephew then of the niece; the sudden decision of the girl to marry, and the insistence of the nephew that he would not live at the house.

'And no reason was ever found to account for the sudden change in the will?' Manson asked at the end of the recital.

'None that I ever knew, and I knew all three persons very well. Eadwin never showed any sign to me that Aelthea was not his favourite — on the contrary.'

'And the will was genuine?'

'There was no doubt that it was Eadwin's signature. I didn't like Rawson and I did like the girl, so on the quiet I got old Swinburne — that's the lawyer — to let me show the will to a handwriting expert. He said there was no doubt that the signature was Eadwin Burstall's.'

'Did Rawson give up the business he said he was engaged in on his uncle's behalf. I thought you said they were going to make a lot of money.'

'I never heard any more of the business. Neither did the lawyer. Mind you, there's nothing in that. William having to earn a living and William with a fortune would be two entirely different people. He wouldn't engage in any work unless the necessity for eating made him do so.'

'What was the business?'

'Haven't the faintest idea. There was no trace of it in Eadwin's papers, so Swinburne told me. I asked him, but neither William nor Eadwin seems to have left anything to explain it. I guess it must have been some kind of a racket for William to have been engaged in it.'

'Well, it's a queer story as you say.'

'I've got a round to attend to,' Forrestal said. 'I'll call for you in the morning and show you some of the fishing water.'

4

Forrestal duly appeared the following morning laden with fishing rods, landing nets and bait cans, and conducted Manson to a pleasant stretch of private water on the Arundel estate. It involved a car ride of a few miles. Fish were obliging — amazingly so. 'Bless my soul,' Forrestal said. 'I've never had such good fishing here.' He eyed the Doctor speculatively. 'Must be the fear of Scotland Yard,' he added humorously. 'The blessed fish have given themselves up!'

The Doctor arrived back at 'Hengeclif' at six o'clock. 'Alice!' he called. 'In the kitchen, darling, talking to Esther.' He walked in, grinning, and planked a 7lb salmon on the table. Alice Manson looked at it, eyes alight. 'A lovely catc — ' She caught herself up and eyed him. 'If you are telling me that you caught this, Harry Manson, I'll call you a . . . a . . . a . . . '

'A what?'

'A malicious perjurer, and you can get three years for perjury. You've told me so yourself. There isn't any salmon water round here. I know that at least.'

'I bought it in Arundel, sweetheart.'

Two hours later with a piece of middle-cut inside him, he felt at peace with the world. The day's effort, however, had tired him, and he decided to spend the evening reading. With that object in view, he carried coffee into the library, and with his wife engaged in needlework, pulled up an armchair to the fire and looked round for a book.

In his general observation of the library collection one odd omission in the liberalism of the owner's choice had caused him momentary curiosity; although most of the arts were represented by volumes, he had noticed that science of any kind appeared to be conspicuous only by its absence. It was as though the reader had eschewed anything modern in any shape or form. Even so, he thought, there should have been in a collection of such dimensions some publication of Science, say such a book as Professor Thompson's

Armchair Science series, or one on modern discoveries. So far he had failed to spot one.

It was, therefore, with surprise that, running his eyes more closely along the lines of shelves he came suddenly, tucked away in a corner, a volume entitled *Inks, Composition and Manufacture*.

'This,' he said to himself, 'is treasure trove, though Hurley and Forrestal would probably not regard it as such on my behalf.'

The scientist, his nerves soothed by the quiet flow of his present ordered life, was feeling the need of a little gentle stimulation in his particular branch of science. Inks and their composition had been one of his studies; he sat down to see what Mitchell had to say on the subject.

After he had turned over some score or so of pages he reached the chapter entitled 'Estimating the Age of Writing.' To his surprise he found a number of passages emphasised by pencil markings down the outside column. Automatically, his eyes went with keen precision over the lines:

'When blue-black ink is freshly applied to the paper (it said) the blue colour will predominate and the ink will appear bright even to the naked eye. But the black iron tannate rapidly forms and gradually masks the blue colour, so that when the ink is examined under the microscope it will appear a deep violet shade.'

A little lower down the page another marked paragraph read:

'Now, if the ink upon a document alleged to be, say, two or three years old, is of a bright blue colour, and is found by chemical test to be of unblotted blue-black iron-gall ink, the fact is at once suspicious.'

Doctor Manson chuckled. 'Very suspicious *indeed*,' he commented. 'As many a person has found out to his cost. Curious,' he said, and laid the book down. 'Now, who in this establishment would be interested in the colour of inks and their age?'

He turned to the frontispiece of the book. 'No signature of the owner. H'm!' He spoke to himself. 'And dated 1937 edition. The last.'

Now, the scientist's chief interest in the study of inks was directed to its use for the purposes of fraud. His knowledge in that direction had been of vital service in his unveiling of the great Stock Exchange share case.[1] He, accordingly, turned presently to that part of Mitchell's *Inks* which related to the investigation of documents, and in particular to the tests applied to cheques, in the strange case of Rex v Pilcher, some years earlier. Reference to the index gave the page as 211.

The page described tests with a reagent upon the signature on cheques drawn by a Mrs. Pilcher, the idea being to prove that a signature on other documents was, in fact, hers. The tests demonstrated by the diffusion reaction of a chemical solution that the signature on the

---

[1] *Crime Pays no Dividends*, by E. and M. A. Radford.

document must have been written about the same time as the signature on one side of the dated cheques. A tick in the margin opposite one paragraph of the description of the test was followed by another marked passage:

If, however, there is pronounced differences between the copying capacity of two parts of the same document, while chemical tests indicate that the inks are of the same type, and the writing is of equal density, it is extremely probable that the two parts were not written at the same time.

'Pretty well certain would be a better conclusion I would have said,' commented Manson. He again sought enlightenment on why the reader should have been interested in consulting Mitchell and so carefully marking certain conclusions. He put the book down and pondered over the problem. It was such outre as these with which the Yard scientist delighted to exercise his brain.

Presently, however, a yawn reminded

him that he had had a strenuous day and was feeling sleepy. He replaced the book on the shelf, and then for no reason at all, retrieved it and laid it on the library table.

The following morning dawned fine and bright, and it was, therefore, with a pleased state of mind that he saw Doctor Forrestal walk up to the front door in golf array. 'Delighted to have a round,' Manson replied to his invitation. 'But how about your patients? I don't want to occupy too much of your time, and I don't want any sudden deaths on my conscience.'

'Don't you worry about that,' retorted Forrestal. I have an arrangement with the hospital and with my surgery that any really urgent message is telephoned to me at the golf club, and if one comes you see, the steward rings the fire bell, and that sets me on the way to the nineteenth hole.'

It was while they were waiting at the tenth, a long hole, for a couple to get ahead, that Manson mentioned the treatise on ink. 'Did your Eadwin Burstall have any hobbies?' he asked.

'Hobbies? What kind of hobby would you be thinking of? He was very keen on his garden.'

'He did not, for instance, take any great interest in ink?'

'Ink?' Forrestal laughed. 'I should say that the only interest Eadwin showed in ink was seeing how little could be used to write down all the household expenses. What makes you think he was interested in ink?'

Manson told him of the book and its marked passages. 'It struck me as curious for a place like 'Hengeclif'. It would not, of course, be curious to find it in my own library. I wondered whether old Eadwin, or his nephew, dabbled in anything in ink?'

'The date of the book, you say, was 1937? Well, it would not be William, for he'd been chucked out by then. And I've never heard of Eadwin being ink conscious. I'll have a look at the book when we get back and see if I can recognise it.'

But inspection of the book after lunch did not supply the answer to Manson's problem. Forrestal, after looking through the pages, said that to the best of his recollection he had never seen it before. He was, he said, pretty well acquainted with the library because he had a habit of looking through the books and borrowing any he thought would prove interesting to him.

'However,' he said, 'the book seems to have been badly treated, and it wasn't like Burstall. He didn't pay good money to spoil books. He was too damned careful.'

'Badly treated? How do you mean?'

Doctor Forrestal showed the book open at the centre. 'It's slightly stained with something that seems to have been spilt over it, and some of the words on other pages have apparently been rubbed right out,' he said. He held the book open for the scientist to inspect.

Doctor Manson took the book over to the window and stared at the pages, which had a slight yellow stain on them. Then he slipped the volume into a jacket pocket. Intrigued, Forrestal looked inquiringly at his host. 'But why the interest, Doctor?' he asked.

'They'd tell you at Scotland Yard

without hesitation, Forrestal,' was the reply. 'The Assistant Commissioner would say it's my suspicious mind. Actually, I have a mind that does not like incongruities, and which sets me off finding the answer to them.'

The ease and lightness of the reply was dropped when the doctor had left. The scientist pulled a desk lamp over towards him. He took the book from his pocket, and inspected the stained page closely. After a long period he moistened a finger and gently rubbed a corner of the stained page. The finger was then put to the tip of his tongue, and the tongue passed round the palate. Next, he paid some attention to the obliterated letters and words on other pages, inspecting them first with the page level in front of his eyes, and then with the lamplight falling obliquely across them. Finally, he closed the book and locked it away in his desk, sat back in the chair and closed his eyes. The broad, high brow broke into furrows, and there appeared little crinkles in the corners of his eyes, while the fingers of his right hand beat an impatient tattoo on the arm of the chair.

After tea he set out down the slope towards the township, and in the main street caught a bus to Littlehampton. In that town Richard Fitzalan in 1346 landed the prisoners from Crecy whose ransoms provided the money for rebuilding his castle, and there Henry VIII built his great Dromions which passed all other great ships of the Commons. He wandered among the shops and, stepping into a chemist's shop, inquired for three articles. The manager shook his head. 'I can do you the test tubes, sir, but not the others,' he said.

'Then I will take the tubes. I do not suppose you sell sodium hypochlorite?'

'No sir. I have never been asked for it.'

'Or oxalic acid?'

'We have a small supply, but I don't suppose we have sold any for months. Did you want some?'

His inquiry for the remaining two articles he required was satisfied at a large dispensing chemist. Bestowing his purchases in a pocket he wended his way back to 'Hengeclif'. After evening dinner he fetched from the kitchen a small kettle with a little water in it and a clean glass. The kettle he set on the fire and when the contents boiled poured a small quantity into the glass allowing it to remain a few moments before emptying it back into the kettle and drying and polishing the glass. He carried out the same operation with one of the test tubes. Then pouring into the glass a little of the contents of two bottles which he had bought in Littlehampton, he mixed them thoroughly, afterwards emptying the contents into the test tube.

Next, he opened the volume on *Inks* at the place where the pages were stained and cut a strip of the discoloured paper from a margin. This he slipped into the test tube, which he corked. After a moment's gentle shaking he inspected the contents under the light of a table lamp. The result seemed to satisfy him, for he emptied the contents into a jug, and washed and dried the glass and the test tube, afterwards placing them in a drawer of the writing table. He made a few notes on a sheet of paper, dated it, and placing it with the tube and the remainder of the chemicals he had used, locked the drawer, switched off the lights and went to bed.

5

It was a strange trait in the character of Doctor Manson as an investigator that so soon as he had solved a problem to his own satisfaction, the problem upon which his energies had devotedly engaged, his interest evaporated completely. Whether the police made an arrest, and if so, whether judge and jury found the accused person innocent or guilty did not interest him in the least; he was convinced in his own mind that the person was beyond all doubt guilty, else he (Manson) would not have brought him to the dock. To his mind those were the only circumstances that mattered; what a jury thought was not evidence.

The explanation was, perhaps, psychological; Harry Manson was gifted, or cursed, with an absorbing curiosity. When the curiosity was satisfied it was as though a current was switched suddenly off an electric motor — the working stopped and refused to restart until the motive power was once more switched on.

The spark which could light his curiosity into activity was a manifold one. It could be coincidence. It could be something out of harmony with its surroundings. Once, in his wanderings he came across a little patch of mint growing in a spot and in soil so foreign to cultivated mint that his curiosity at this apparent trick of nature had caused him to take a sample of the soil and preserve it. Months later the sample led to a murder charge, and a hanging.

It was this unbelief in discord that led to his curiosity in the copy of *Inks, Composition and Manufacture* because it seemed to his ordered mind out of harmony with the remainder of the library. That the stained pages should be in the book of a man who took care of his books, and in a way that was itself a curiosity, formed a coincidence to which the Doctor felt he could not subscribe. That was the reason for his investigation. One part of the curiosity had been satisfied; his experiments of the evening had told him what was the cause of the stain. But the presence of the book still continued to worry him.

It was at this stage that a chance departure from customary routine started him off on a new trail. It was his practice after a morning stroll to pass through the front garden gate of the house and re-enter the house by the front door. On this occasion he varied the rule by taking a short cut up a path passing through the private gate in the high wall surrounding the property, and walking to the French windows of the library which stood open to the sun.

His light-soled shoes made no noise on the path. He was about to enter the room when he saw that it already had an occupant; a woman was standing at the far shelves of the library engaged in rummaging hurriedly through books. She had not, apparently, heard his quiet approach. Doctor Manson regarded the operation with some astonishment. He found himself in two minds as to what course to take, but decided that to enter the library now would undoubtedly be a source of embarrassment to a visitor, whoever she might be, caught rummaging in the room of a tenant of the house. Accordingly, he walked round the house and entered as usual by the front door.

Pausing only to hang his hat in the hall, he walked on to the library and opened the door. The action was followed by a thud and sound of scuffling. He hesitated for a moment to allow the visitor to compose herself, and then entered. To his surprise, the room was empty. A quick glance at the window, however, was in time to give him a fleeting glance of a skirt vanishing round the lintel. He crossed to the windows. To his astonishment there was no sign of the visitor; the garden was empty of any trespasser.

'Curiouser and curiouser, as Lewis Carroll would say,' he muttered. 'Where the deuce has she gone?' He stepped out and walked the width of the house, and to the garden gate; there was no sign of the intruder. Returning, he inspected that part of the library at which he had seen the woman on his approach. A book was lying on the floor. 'Obviously the little thud,' he said to himself, and picked it up. It was a copy of the *Ovid*.

He smiled rather grimly. 'I don't suppose she came here looking for the *Ovid*,' he said. 'Then what the devil *was* she looking for?' He eyed the books on the shelf which had hitherto been as straight and level as a parade of guardsmen, but were now as ragged as an awkward squad. 'H'm, Hammerton's *Masterpieces of Eloquence*, *Platt's Last Rambles in Classics*, *Ten Thousand Curious Things* — nothing to explain her presence here, except that now we have ten thousand *and one* curious things. I give it up.'

He replaced the copy of *Ovid* in the shelf and straightened the row of books. The result showed that nothing had been taken from the shelf; there were no blank spaces. 'Whatever she wanted, she hasn't got it,' he decided, and sat down to think out the mystery.

A knock at the door interrupted his deliberations. To his invitation Esther entered. 'Sorry to trouble you, sir,' she said, 'but Miss Whiting who lived here would like to see you for a minute if you can spare the time. She has arrived quite unexpectedly.'

'But, of course, Esther. I shall be most pleased to meet Miss Whiting. Bring her along by all means.' 'Well, well,' he said mentally, as the girl came into the room, 'the mysterious visitor in person.' Aloud, he greeted, 'I am delighted to know you, Miss Whiting.' He was, in fact more delighted than his expression could convey.

'I am sorry to intrude upon you, Mr. Manson,' she announced. 'You probably know nothing whatever about me.'

'On the contrary, I can say that you are the cousin of my present landlord, and the niece of the late Mr. Eadwin Burstall,' the Doctor said with a smile. He seated her in an armchair. 'Now, what can I do for you?'

'I should have written you beforehand. You see, when I went away I left a number of my personal things until I made plans for the future. I am now pretty well sure of my movements. I am, in fact, being married, so thought I had better gather my things together, pick out those things I intend to take with me, and dispose of the rest.'

'Most desirable.'

'Therefore I hope you would not mind my being in the house for a few hours and have a meal with Esther. I want to look up one or two friends I shall probably never see again.'

'No doubt you include Doctor Forrestal among them. He is due here very shortly for lunch with me. I hope you will do me the honour of sharing the meal with us. Then you can make your final parting fortified with a sufficiency of lamb and green peas.'

It was Forrestal who, during the meal, introduced the topic of the lost inheritance of Miss Whiting. Doctor Manson blessed him for it. He had been racking his brain to know how to bring the conversation round without showing any inquisitiveness.

'You know, Doctor, all of us round here expected we would have been the guest of Aelthea on an occasion such as this,' Doctor Forrestal explained after the table had been cleared and coffee served. 'That is, of course, no reflection on your hospitality,' he added.

Doctor Manson grinned delightedly. 'Of course not. I should have been delighted to sit at this table as Miss Whiting's guest.' He turned towards her. 'Forrestal told me of the circumstances of the death of your uncle and the remarkable disclosures that followed it,' he explained. 'On the face of what he has told me you would appear to have been ungenerously treated by the late Mr. Burstall.'

'Well, of course, it *was* uncle's money and he could do what he liked with it. But I must say that I felt a little hurt and resentful at the way in which he did it.'

'Have you any idea why he should play so dastardly a trick on you — a slight quarrel which rankled, perhaps?'

'There was never any quarrel, I assure you.'

'He might have been in fear of your leaving him, and allowed you to think you were his heiress in order that you would remain with him?'

'I do not think he ever thought that of later years — that I would take another, less domestic, position. He had discouraged my ideas of employment, and I had long ceased to suggest it.'

'The last time they were mentioned — when would that be?'

'Perhaps three or four years back.' Doctor Manson thought back. 'That would be before the date this newest and latest will was made, and that would dispose of the possibility of undue influence by the nephew; he had not come back into favour. There is left the possibility of your uncle's state of mind. You were most in contact with him, Miss Whiting. Did you see any signs of mental decay? Was your uncle, for instance, forgetful of things? Doctor Forrestal will know what I mean when I ask whether he forgot something that happened yesterday, but remembered everything that occurred in his boyhood? That is one of the signs of *senile dementia*.'

'I can assure you he remembered things perfectly — for instance which week I spent more than he liked to spend.'

'Forrestal?'

'Not a sign. He was his own unpleasant self up to a day before he died. He cursed me for a liar because I told him I had dropped in to see him while on the way to a patient. He announced that he had heard Aelthea telephone for me.'

'Is the reason for his quarrel with his nephew known?'

Miss Whiting shook her head. 'No, but I did hear that it was something about a cheque.'

'I take it you do not know what the business was he was engaged in?'

'All I know is that it was something secret and not to be talked about.'

After the departure of his visitors, Doctor Manson set out in tabulated form the morning's queer happenings. They read:

(1) Knowing he was absent from the house, Miss Whiting visited the library room, hunting for something, apparently a book. No book is missing, so she seemingly did not find it.

(2) Yet, when she asked permission to be in the house to collect her personal belongings she made no mention of the book she had gone to find. The book she wanted was obviously urgently needed otherwise she would not have risked being in the library to get it.

(3) The book must be something she does not want to be seen with, otherwise she would have taken the opportunity of asking if she may take it.

(4) Her story that she had come to collect a few personal things was suspicious because when she left the house to return to London, she carried nothing but her handbag.

He put the notes away in a locked drawer, then, turning to the bookshelves in which the girl had been interested, he pushed the books back half-an-inch in the depth of the shelves, so that they were out of alignment with the books in the remaining shelves.

The artful dodge came off. When, just before dinner, he returned to the house after going to the pillar box to post a letter, he found Esther leaving the library with a duster in her hand — and nothing else. His eyes dropped to the duster and remained there. Esther, in a voice in which confusion was cleverly and quickly disguised as anger, said: 'I've been dusting round. The slipshod way girls work today is disgraceful.'

Inside the library he went across to the shelves, and smiled grimly. The titles had been rearranged on the shelves he had prepared and the books were now level with those elsewhere. Moreover the ragged arrangement of other shelves showed that they, also, had been examined.

He sat down at a desk and wrote a letter, afterwards carrying it to the postbox. Dinner was taken that evening with the door of the dining-room open, facing the open door of the library, and afterwards he did not leave again from the time coffee was served until he went to bed. When he retired the library door was locked, and the key safely in his pocket.

6

Detective-Chief-Inspector James Merry looked across at his Chief, saw the right hand resting on the chair in which Doctor Manson was sitting. Its long, sensitive fingers were beating a tattoo on the arm. He knew the signs

'Are you working, Harry?' he demanded.

Doctor Manson opened his eyes. 'What the . . . ' he began: looked up, following the line of his companion's eyes, saw his unconsciously tapping fingers, and ceased it.

'I don't quite know, Jim,' he said.

Merry is the Deputy Scientist of Scotland Yard, in charge of the Laboratory. He had made the journey to Cissing at Doctor Manson's invitation to spend a few days, 'and bring your golf clubs with you.' Alice Manson, he explained, had had to return to their home in Berkeley Square, where her father had been taken ill; he was over 80 years of age.

'Well, I *do* know,' Merry retorted. 'What is it, Harry?'

'So far . . . nothing. But . . . you know why I came down here. I wanted a complete rest from thinking. And for a fortnight I found it. Then queer things began to happen . . . '

'And your suspicious mind began to piece them together! I know.'

'Something of the sort, Jim.' He rose and from a locked drawer took out the book on inks. 'The first of them was this.' He passed the book over.

Merry turned over the pages, read the marked passages, came to the cut margins and examined their edges.

'New,' he said. 'Your doings, Harry?'

'Mine.'

'Then you know what the stain is?'

'Sodium hypochlorite, medium strength.'

'What else is there about it?'

'Only the book itself.' Manson waved a hand towards the bookshelves, and Merry after a moment's thought, rose and crossed to them. He came back to the chair. 'You mean it doesn't fit, I suppose?'

'So I thought.'

'Who owned it?'

'Presumably a man named Eadwin Burstall. He's dead. He left about £100,000. And two wills,' he added, thoughtfully. 'The lawyer read the wrong one.'

'I'd better have the background, Harry.' Manson told him and Merry considered it in silence.

'Do you think this is the book for which the girl was searching? You had it in your desk, you remember.'

'I do *not* think so. Had it have been she would have known the title and would not have found it necessary to go rummaging among the shelves.'

'That's true. Did she find the book she wanted, do you know?'

'She left here without it. My little deception showed that. Esther — that's the housekeeper — was looking for it after she had gone. I asked Esther if Miss Whiting had found the book she wanted, and she said she had. Since then, there's been another searcher.'

'You don't say! Who's the third johnny?'

'Doctor Forrestal. He came here to run the rule over me, spent two minutes on it and ten minutes looking through the books because he wanted to borrow a good one. He had previously failed to display any enthusiasm for the books, and he is, incidentally, a close friend of Miss Whiting, and left with her after her unfruitful visit.'

'I see.' Merry pointed an accusing finger. 'And you've got me down here to help you go through this jungle' — waving his pipe at the bookshelves. 'There'll be' — he made a mental calculation — 'about two thousand ruddy books here. The lady knew for what she was hunting, and couldn't find it. We haven't the least idea what we want and we're going to look for it. Suffering saints!'

Doctor Manson knocked the dottle from his pipe — for he treated his favourite briar delicately — slowly refilled it before replying. 'Your recitation approaches the hyperbolical, Jim,' he retorted. 'The incomprehensible may not turn out to be as complex as your erudition would seem to infer. It is true that we do not know for what we are searching. But we *do* know for what we are *not* searching, and a negative is sometimes as good a clue as a positive. It is so in this case.'

'Most enlightening. Then what is it we are *not* nosing round for like a couple of ferrets?'

'A book.' The Doctor, a twinkle in his eye, watched the effect of the pronouncement on his colleague.

'We're going to search through a library of two thousand books because we don't want a book . . . '

'Let us apply a little of the logic of our late lamented friend, Mr. Jevons, to the case. Aelthea Whiting was looking against time for something in these shelves. I suggest it was not for a book she was searching. What is the evidence against?' He walked to the shelves. 'Now, there are the rows of shelves through which she was struggling.' He read out the titles: 'The *Ovid, Socrates, History of Classical Scholarship, Greek Studies,* and suchlike. Would you run berserk to assimilate the contents of any one of these when, if you were so minded, you could borrow a copy from any public library?'

'Conceded. What, then, have we left from Jevons?'

'I should say the *contents* of a book.'

'You mean something not belonging to the book itself — something extraneous . . . put into it?'

'For safety, of course, yes. Or for an urgently required suddenly necessary hiding place. I'm theorising now, but I have little doubt it is good theorising because I can think of nothing else that fits the circumstances. Miss Whiting did not know which book she wanted. I think the reason is, that, while engaged on something of a private nature, she was suddenly disturbed and that she slipped the something that was in her hands into the first book she came to, and that she had not time to note the title of the book. She seemed to think that the book was one in the shelves I have indicated and which she also indicated by the fact that she went through them . . . '

'Somebody has found the something and nicked it, eh?' Merry said.

'Or somebody has by chance moved

the book to somewhere else in the shelves.'

'Quite. Which means we've to go through the lot of them. Any idea as to what the something may be?'

'Only that it is an extraneous article which would not declare itself to casual inspection.'

'A paper, possibly?'

'So. At a rough guess, Jim, I would say we are looking for a piece, or at the outside several pieces, of paper which, slipped between the pages of a book, would not betray themselves by parting the leaves.'

The search took them into the early hours of the morning. Each book was held by the spine and shaken. 'I hate treating books in this way,' Manson said, 'but it is the most likely way of discovering anything between the leaves. By 2.30 they had reached the bookshelves nearest the fireplace. A number of pieces of paper had fallen from books, but proved to be nothing more than book-marks. Merry pulled out a book, shook it and paper fell to the floor. 'Aha, what has the brazen Jade presented us with this time?' he asked.

The find was a pinned-together combination of three sheets of thin paper. The sheets appeared to have been torn from a writing pad with a pin at the top left-hand corner. Doctor Manson read the first few words on the top sheet — and stiffened. Merry crossed to his side and pored over his shoulders. He whistled softly, a long shrill note of surprise.

The writing was in pencil. 'HB and cheap,' Merry commented. 'Look how it goes to a scratch here and there. That means there is stone in the graphite, and you don't get that in good pencils.'

'We can say that the writing anyway, has been carefully and deliberately done. The 'i's' are conscientiously dotted and the 't's' crossed. He read it out, slowly:

ACONITINE: With small doses the heart is unaffected. In larger quantities the pulse rate is quickened. But if more is given the force becomes less and the pulse is slowed. The respiration centre becomes depressed.

BENZACONINE: Better. Does not cause tingling or numbness of mucuous surfaces. In larger doses slows the heart beat, its action being in the heart muscle itself. Causes a semi-comatose condition.

VERONAL: Soluble in water and readily absorbed. Causes depression of the respiratory and circulatory systems and a fall to a marked degree in the blood pressure. Produces a condition of confusion which may lead the patient to take a number of tablets without intending to do so. Death has occurred after sixty grains.

HASHISH: Small doses make a person pleased with himself, cheerful and talkative. The heart is accelerated. Used to excess it causes degeneration of the central nervous system.

PHYSOSTIGMINE: Diminishes the rate of the heart beat. Paralyses the motor centre of the brain and causes death by paralysis in the respiratory centre in the medulla. The pulse becomes slow and feeble and the action of the heart may be irregular.

VERATRINE: Makes pulse feeble and irregular, and respiration slow.

DIGITALIS: Makes the pulse rate slow and irregular. The respiration becomes slow and sighing, and the patient becomes drowsy.

The Aconitine and the Benzaconine entries filled the entire first of the three slips. Having read the page, Doctor Manson produced a pair of tweezers from a waistcoat pocket and with these clipped and lifted the sheet exposing to view the second page which contained the Veronal and Hashish notes. The same procedure revealed the third page. The reading concluded, he restored the slips to their original form, still with the tweezers and without touching the pages with his fingers edged them into a large envelope and sealed it.

'My word, Harry,' Merry said. 'How

did your ex-landlord die?'

'So far as I know, naturally. He was a patient of Sir Charles Hurley. Don't jump to hasty conclusions. The note may be some of the contents of the book, though I don't remember seeing anything of the kind. What was the title of the book from which they dropped?'

Merry retrieved it from the shelf. '*The Handbook of Folklore* by C. C. Burns,' he announced. 'Doesn't sound much like a treatise on poisons to me.'

'No more it is. But we still have no proof that this is that for which we are looking. We must go through the remainder of the books.'

Nothing else came to light.

7

It was not until Manson and Merry were well into a morning walk that any reference was made to the discovery of the previous night. For one thing the scientist did not want any inkling of his activities to be noised abroad; an overheard word might be distorted and magnified into an altogether false premise. If there *was* anything question-able in the happenings in 'Hengeclif, it was pretty certain that someone in the house knew something about it; the search by Esther in the library proved that.

For three-quarters of an hour the two had walked in silence, except for an observation by one or other of them on a rural curiosity or aspect of interest. Then Merry broached the subject. 'What are you going to make of all this, Harry?' he asked.

'So far as I can see at present, there is

nothing we *can* make of it Jim. What have we? Two circumstances which seem to you and I rather queer . . . '

'Suspicious would be my word for it.'

'Well, suspicious if you prefer it. But are they suspicious to anyone but ourselves? We have that kind of mind. Suppose we put all we have in front of Stiffy[1] and explain that they are very suspicious because the book on inks was the only one of its kind in the library, and the descriptions of poisons are suspicious because someone was searching for something we don't know what in the library. What is he going to say?'

'He wouldn't say anything. Stiffy would snort and blow the pince-nez off the end of his nose.'

'Exactly. I don't like the look of things at all. Maybe it's a kind of instinct with me; maybe it's imagination engendered by the fact that I have a suspicious mind. But until we can accumulate a few more facts

---

[1] Mr. Horace Abigail, Home Office Pathological expert, known to Yard officers as 'Stiffy' for obvious reasons.

— and I emphasise the word facts — we have no justification for thinking that there is anything that concerns us at all. Suppose you tell me what kind of tale is told you by the book and the slips of paper — and what you know of certain circumstances.'

* * *

Merry thought for a moment or two. Then: 'I do not think that the inanimate objects represented by the ink book and the papers can begin to tell us anything until we have the key. As I see it — and I thought about it all night, when I should have been keeping up my health and strength by sleeping — there is one missing link in the story you've told me of the Burstall family.'

'Missing link? Elaborate.'

'There were, you say, three wills. In the original made by Eadwin Burstall, the nephew inherited half the estate, subject to legacies to Miss Whiting and the servants. The second was drawn up by the solicitor, and under it the nephew got the order of the boot and the estate went to the niece. And the third was the one found by the solicitor after the funeral, in which the nephew got the estate almost completely. Now we know of the present *existence* of two of the wills — the second and the third. What became of the first one?'

Manson looked up sharply. 'According to Swinburne — the lawyer — it was returned to Burstall when the second will was drawn up by the lawyer. He asked for it back — Burstall, I mean.'

'Is it still in existence, or was it in existence immediately prior to the death of the old man?'

'I have no idea. What is at the back of your mind?'

'If the will was not destroyed, but was kept by Burstall and cannot now be found — does that convey anything to your imagination?'

'Yes.' Manson smiled. 'But that tale won't talk, Jim. Swinburne, the lawyer, told Doctor Forrestal, who saw your point at the time, that the new will favouring Rawson was *not* on all fours with the earlier will in his favour. The figure of Miss Whiting's legacy was out by a considerable amount in comparison, and she also had half the residue.'

'So you told me, I remember. It does not altogether negate what I am thinking. Do you recall the Bridger case and the Kerford will suit?'

Manson whistled softly. The old alert look crept over his face, and the crinkles appeared in the corners of his eyes. 'I wonder,' he said, softly, 'I wonder. But how the deuce are we going to find out? The only person who could possibly help is Swinburne himself, and we can't ask him. We haven't any authority and he would refuse to answer in any case.'

'He seemed from what you have described to me to be very annoyed about the change in the will. I gathered he was rather in favour of Miss Whiting and replied tartly to remarks by the nephew. If he thought there was a prospect of upsetting the will would he be inclined, do you think, to talk a little?'

Doctor Manson walked on in silence for a few moments. Then: 'He's a friend of Forrestal . . . I'll see what the doctor can do.'

★ ★ ★

It happened, however, that before any progress could be made in the way of information from Mr. Swinburne a new light was thrown on the library discoveries. It was a stumbling block to the scientist that the book on inks was itself no evidence of any kind against any occupant of the house. Some of the books they had examined in the library had on their flyleaves inscriptions other than Burstall; these, it was clear to the Doctor had been purchased, probably in bulk from second-hand book-dealers at some time in order to fill gaps in the shelves. It is a practice adopted by many owners of libraries who, as they acquire more books of their own, gradually sell out the bought 'spares'. He had been cognisant of the fact that the volume, the marked paragraphs of which had excited his curiosity, might well have been included in such purchases. It was not likely, he admitted, since it was the only book of its kind, and dealers generally arranged such sales in order of subjects, but it was still a possibility.

As a result Merry and he turned up a number of pages in the *Encyclopaedia Britannica* which occupied a bottom shelf in the library. They found to their satisfaction that certain paragraphs relating to the use and qualities of ink were marginally marked in the same way as paragraphs in Mitchell's book.

'That makes it pretty obvious that the book was used and belonged to someone in the household,' said Manson with a justifiable satisfaction at his hunch. He decided to push his luck further. Merry turned up Aconitine in the *Encyclopaedia*. The reference contained no annotations. Similar failure was met with the case of Digitalis and Hashish. But when Venatrine and Veronal were turned up there was a different tale to tell.

'*Touché*,' called Merry at the Venatrine entry. Doctor Manson crossed and inspected the page. Two small lines of emphasis were drawn in the margin opposite the description of the physical effects of the drug. 'Very satisfactory,' Manson said. 'Now try Veronal.' Once again, two or three paragraphs were emphasised. 'Which shows that the papers of written memoranda, too, were done in this household. We seem to be getting a little further, Harry, eh?'

Manson nodded, walked to the desk and extracted from the envelope the slips of paper found in the *Handbook of Folklore* and compared the notes with the marked passages in the *Britannica*. They did not agree except in one instance. 'In other words,' he said, 'the writer had some other source of information of which we have not yet any knowledge.' He thought for a moment. 'Let us visit the nearest public library.'

Inquiries there, however, had little success. The library possessed no standard works on poisons of any kind, not even *Black's Medical Dictionary*. 'We have no call for them,' the head of the reference section said. She suggested that they might find copies at Brighton Library. Merry journeyed there without any success. No copies of Bamford, or of Blyth, or Glaister showed any marked passages.

Doctor Manson, nearer at home, had more success. He visited Doctor Forrestal to suggest that he and Mr. Swinburne should join Merry and he for dinner, on a convenient evening, and had taken occasion to compliment Forrestal on his collection of medical books. He took down a Bamford and turned over the pages; they were completely unmarked. Blyth was similarly clean but in Hale White's *Materia Medica* he found four markings each of which was a more detailed account than the *précis* on the notepad slips. Merry and he browsed over the fact that evening.

'And Forrestal, you said, was going through the shelves here on one occasion, Harry. I suppose the *Materia* was not here at the time and was taken away by him? That may have been the book for which Miss Whiting was searching.'

'You mean it may have been not for herself but for him she was searching? It won't hold water. Why should she be in such a stew about his book when he could walk into the place, tell me he had lent the book to Burstall and just put it into his pocket and walk off with it? Anyway, had it been here at the time, I think I should have noticed it.'

In the collection of dull-covered books the *Materia* would have forced attention; its covers are a bright hue of green.

★   ★   ★

Mr. Swinburne crumpled his napkin, laid it beside his plate and patted his stomach complacently. 'That, Doctor Manson, is the best meal I have had for many a long day, if I may say so,' he announced.

Doctor Manson acknowledged the compliment. 'I will pass it on to Esther, Mr. Swinburne. She cooked it. But you must have had a long experience of Esther's cooking by this time.'

'True, sir. But, alas, Esther in those days did not have the kind of materials for the feast you have provided. My old friend Burstall was not the man to invest money in ducks and trimmings; he preferred to invest in less substantial things.'

'But showing a more profitable aftermath,' put in Doctor Forrestal, and a grin ran round the company as they moved to the library for coffee.

The dinner party had been preceded by much activity. Merry had the previous day driven to Scotland Yard to deal with any matter of moment which could not be handled by Wilkins, the Laboratory chief assistant. He had instructions to procure several items which Doctor Manson thought might be needed if the dinner went the way he hoped; his return to 'Hengeclif' was accompanied by a case of bottles which had been carefully packed in the back of the Rolls. He carried them into the house and then took from the roomy bucket of the car what appeared to be a species of camera, and several other bulky objects. Finally, he dived into the car and produced a leather case. Manson eyed it, questioningly.

'Just in case, Harry. You never know. I smuggled it out unseen so nobody will have any suspicion.' It was Doctor

Manson's portable laboratory, referred to in the Yard as 'The Box of Tricks', and was in evidence only when the doctor was in a hunt. Manson nodded his appreciation of its presence, and locked it in a wardrobe of his bedroom. Then the pair discussed the possibilities of the coming dinner party.

'I have no definite plans,' the Doctor said. 'We will see how the chatter develops, but I shall try to steer it into the channels we want. But one word of warning — we must keep clear of any mention of poison. If Forrestal is concerned at all — even merely as a friendly helper of Miss Whiting to recover some possession of hers — he'll be on his guard if we introduce poison, however innocently. Let us keep to the three wills.'

A bowl of fruit and a silver container of nuts awaited the party in the library. Doctor Manson poured from a decanter a glass of wine for each of his guests and one for himself. Mr. Swinburne took a sip at his wine and started in surprise. 'By gad, Doctor Manson, this is a remarkably fine port,' he said. He took another sip.

'Don't tell me it's '96.'

Manson eyed him. 'Fortunately I have a modest supply which is kept for special occasions. This is such a one.'

'God bless my soul, Forrestal, this is the pinnacle of good host-elry, if I may use the word 'host' in its proper meaning — that he will bring sixty miles, port from his own cellar.' He looked round the room lit by a tall standard lamp that threw a radiance over the immediate neighbourhood but left a shadow hovering over the ranks of books along the wall. 'This, Forrestal, is a very different gathering to the last one at which you and I were present in this room, eh?'

Manson looked across at Merry and received his satisfied wink. 'That, I suppose would have been after the death of your late client, my ex-landlord?' he said.

'Indeed, yes, Doctor. We had just returned from conveying his mortal remains to the tomb . . . '

'And just disposed, too, of his mortal *estate* — twice,' interrupted Doctor Forrestal.

'Twice!' Merry looked incredulity.

'Alas, sir, twice is correct.' Forrestal shook his head regretfully.

'Well, since he couldn't have been twins unless he was Siamese twins how did that come about?' Merry settled down to hear the answer, winking at his chief sitting on the blind side of the lawyer.

'Doctor Manson, it was the most regrettable thing that could possibly happen to a lawyer. You being what you are, will be able to appreciate the position.'

'I have heard only the bare outlines, and that at second hand, but I gather that your late client left you with one will and left another to be found after you had disclosed to the benefactors the one in your possession.'

'Most reprehensible.' Mr. Swinburne shook his silver-domed head. 'Let me tell you as a lawyer to a man of law . . . '

Doctor Manson replenished the glasses. Mr. Swinburne took another sample drink and then settled again in his armchair. 'As I was going to say it was the most reprehensible . . . '

For a quarter of an hour the old lawyer reminisced on the story of the two wills. Doctor Manson listened in silence to the end. Mr. Swinburne eyed him anxiously at the conclusion. 'Now, what do you say of a thing like that, sir?'

The scientist turned his cigar round in his fingers before replying. He eyed the tale-teller in silent thought. 'It is indeed a very strange story, Mr. Swinburne,' he said at last. 'I take it you do not altogether approve of the last of the wills?'

'Approve? My dear sir, the terms were a disgrace to the memory of Eadwin Burstall. God bless my soul, Aelthea Whiting devoted years of her life to Eadwin. And this place was her home — her only home. Common gratitude should have moved him to leaving her at least this house, whatever he did with the remainder of his estate. I have sometimes wondered . . . ' His voice faded into silence, but he pulled thoughtfully at his cigar.

'Wondered?' Doctor Manson put in a reminding query.

'Well, perhaps I ought not to put it

quite like that. I am the family lawyer. But we are speaking under the rose, and we are professional men akin to each other. What I have occasionally wondered was whether Eadwin meant it that way.'

'You mean there was some jiggery-pokery?' Forrestal substituted for the law's nicety of language the straight talk of fact.

'John always led me to believe that Aelthea was his favourite, even on the day when he told me to pay William Rawson £10 a week. And that, you understand was only a few weeks before his death.'

'What! I didn't know that,' burst out Forrestal.

The lawyer looked his surprise. 'It's hardly a thing a lawyer would disclose while his client was still alive, is it?'

Doctor Manson heard the casual mention of the income with agitated surprise. He now sought to elaborate it. 'Do I understand, Mr. Swinburne, that your late client was still speaking in high terms of his niece so soon before his death, and at precisely the same time that he had taken his nephew back into a certain amount of favour?'

'That is so.'

'And was the nephew living in the house at the time the request was made to you to pay him ten pounds a week?'

'Oh dear, yes. It was after he returned to the house. Eadwin told me it was a salary for the business he was doing with him.'

'So that it was after he had made out the last of the wills leaving him the estate — and he was yet regarding Miss Whiting with satisfaction, in fact, admiration?'

The lawyer regarded the scientist with some surprise. 'The point had not struck me, Doctor Manson,' he said. 'Let me think . . . er . . . 'em . . . Yes, the facts are correct. To the best of my recollection it was made clear that the last will, under which Rawson benefitted, was drawn up and dated prior to his returning to 'Hengeclif'.'

'This seems to be a new but very important development. Apart from the handwriting expert of Doctor Forrestal's acquaintance, no other examination of the will was made, I take it?'

'No. On the face of the decision of the expert there seemed no point in further examination, Doctor. The advice was quite definite, was it not, Forrestal?'

The doctor nodded. 'Not a doubt about it,' he said.

'Is the will still in your possession, Mr. Swinburne?'

'Yes. The young rascal of a nephew took no further interest. He was not even sufficiently interested to live in this beautiful house — the old man's main request. All Eadwin's personal possessions were moved when you came into occupation, and are in my possession awaiting the nephew's instructions.'

'In going through them — I suppose they were in the desk here — ' The lawyer nodded agreement — 'You did not, I suppose, come across the copy of the first will?'

'First will? You mean the one by which the estate was left to Miss Whiting? I had that one with me.'

'No, Mr. Swinburne I mean the earlier one in which the estate was divided between them.'

'Bless me, of course. I had forgotten about that one. No, it was certainly not among the papers. Fancy me never thinking of that.'

'Quite conceivable, Mr. Swinburne. There is no reason why you should. Talking over the story with us and my questions to you, will have brought the matter to the recollection of all who knew about it. Anyhow, the thing that matters is that it was not there. Perhaps Mr. Burstall took your advice and thought it best to destroy it to avoid accidents, eh? Another glass of port for everybody?'

Doctor Manson settled his guests in renewed good humour with a drink and fresh cigars before he ventured on the point for which he had engineered the dinner. He addressed the old lawyer. 'This has been extraordinarily interesting to me, Mr. Swinburne,' he said. 'I have had extensive experience of strange testamentary documents, but none so bizarre as this, and its attendant complications for you. I wonder whether, as a matter of interest, I could see and examine these two wills. They would, I am sure, afford you and myself an interesting half-an-hour.'

Mr. Swinburne hesitated. 'It is a little unusual, Doctor Manson,' he said. 'I do not quite know . . .'

'Then say no more about it. I would not cause you any embarrassment for the world.'

'No, I think, perhaps . . . There is nothing really private about these documents. I think no harm could be done and no confidences broken by an inspection of this kind between friends. The wills have been publicly read.'

'That is exceedingly kind of you. Then may I suggest you bring them tomorrow morning, if that is convenient to you. Say about eleven o'clock, which is a good time for a pre-luncheon glass of port.'

With the guests departed, Merry executed a highland fling. 'What intuition on my part to bring the Box of Tricks!' he said.

'Keep your exuberance for after the event, Jim.' Doctor Manson was always cautious where an unknown quantity was concerned. 'But I agree this is an unexpected piece of good fortune, due, I think, mostly to the port. If there is anything in your hint we ought to be able to find it out while the will is in our hands.'

8

Punctually at eleven o'clock Mr. Swinburne walked up the drive, knocked at the door of 'Hengeclif' and was shown, according to instructions, into the library. He took a bundle of papers from a side pocket of his coat and placed them on the table.

After aperitifs had been taken, Doctor Manson picked up the bundle of papers. 'These, I assume, Mr. Swinburne, are the two wills?' he commented.

'They are, Doctor, I am anxious to see just how a scientific examination, such as you suggested, is actually performed. I have many times read your expert evidence on what transpired from such examinations; this will be seeing from behind the scenes, as it were.'

'Well, I cannot, of course, guarantee any results which will surprise you with the magic of science. This is more in the way of an interesting experiment to me, as I hope it will be to you.' He was opening the papers as he spoke. They consisted of two envelopes with enclosures. Doctor Manson looked at the first of them. It was a plain foolscap envelope of heavy paper with the inscription in typewriting on the outside, 'Last will and testament of Eadwin Burstall.'

'One of your own envelopes, I take it?' Doctor Manson queried.

Mr. Swinburne nodded. 'Why?' he asked.

'Too good a quality for Burstall, Swinburne. Must have cost at least sixpence; and you tell me that he was a careful man.'

The lawyer regarded the scientist with delighted amusement. 'A psychologist,' he said.

Manson was extracting a will from the envelope. 'No. Just common perception,' he retorted. 'And observation. It is strange how little observation is practiced by the average person. This, I take it, is the will which you read out to the gathering in this room?'

He ran rapidly through the wording

and after a moment or two laid it aside and took up a second envelope, looking inquiringly at the lawyer.

'That is the final will, Doctor.'

Manson nodded and extracted the second of the wills from its receptacle, and laid it on the table. Then, taking a lens from a waistcoat pocket, he subjected the envelope to a careful examination. It was a standard size 9″ × 4″ but white and not cream-laid. Written across the front and centred in the width were the words: 'My last Will and Testament'. Manson looked across at Swinburne.

'Eadwin Burstall's writing, Doctor,' he said. 'The man told the truth at the third attempt,' he added in jest at the three wills.

'That still remains to be seen. Where has this envelope been kept since it came into your possession?'

'In the deed box of the Burstall family.'

Once more he inspected the envelope through his lens and afterwards carried out a similar examination of an envelope containing a letter from Mr. Burstall to the lawyer. That operation concluded, he placed them side by side on the table and drew forward a desk lamp so that the light shone evenly on the pair. 'The filter lens, Merry,' he asked.

The Deputy Scientist opened the Box of Tricks and from it handed a large oblong-shaped glass in a frame. Doctor Manson peered through it at the envelopes.

Mr. Swinburne, who had watched the performance on the envelopes without wills so far having engaged the attention of the scientist, felt himself constrained to break the silence. 'I thought you looked for fingerprints with the use of powder, Doctor,' he said. 'I fear the envelopes have been handled by too many people now to be of any use for prints.'

'Yes, I fear they would be. But it is not fingerprints in which I am interested, Mr. Swinburne. The lens is merely a screen to give me the colour tones of the two envelopes. Tell me, did Eadwin Burstall keep his notepaper, etc. in his desk?'

'He did, Doctor.'

'Open desk?'

'Open! God bless my soul,' Mr.

Swinburne exploded. 'Dear me, Eadwin never left anything open, not even a book of postage stamps.'

'I see. When I took over this house the desk was plentifully provided with paper and envelopes. Can you tell me whether the paper and envelopes are those usually used by Mr. Burstall — I mean did you purchase any more, or give orders for any paper to be bought?'

'I can say that they are the paper and envelopes that were being used by Eadwin up to his death. And I can say that for the simple reason that after his death black-edged paper was obtained by Miss Whiting, and that alone was used by the household.'

Doctor Manson crossed to the desk and returned with a foolscap envelope. He compared it with the two already examined. He said nothing, however, but placed it with the other. Then, for the first time he took up the will under which William Rawson had inherited his uncle's estate. 'I think we will photograph this first — that is, with your permission, Mr. Swinburne.'

'In for a penny, in for a pound,' the lawyer replied with a wave of a hand. 'But why photograph it when you have the original?'

'For the same reason that you wear spectacles. Because it magnifies your vision and enables you to see small things that may not be visible to the unaided eyesight. Faults in writing or alterations carefully made in a document are not obtrusive in the small original, but when enlarged up to say, four or five magnifications they are very obtrusive indeed.'

Merry had already set up a camera, one of the cased objects which he had brought down from London with the bottles of port. The will was mounted on an easel and the rays of a portable floodlight directed on it. The document was focussed on the ground glass of the camera and an exposure given. Merry removed the plateholder and went off to the bathroom to develop the negative under cover of the black linen folds of his development bag.

With his departure Doctor Manson cleared a space on the library table which he proceeded to cover with a sheet of white, glazed paper taken from the Box of Tricks. On this he deposited a porcelain tile, a number of small bottles and a powerful electric torch.

'Ha!' exclaimed Mr. Swinburne. 'We appear to be coming to something.' He watched the scientist lay the will flat on the table, read carefully through the document, and finally examine various parts of the writing through his lens.

'Well,' Swinburne said, with a grin. 'I should say you have exhausted the last grain of meaning from the terms of the bequests.' Manson smiled and put away the lens. 'It is the hidden meaning for which I am searching,' he replied. He flicked on the light in an electric torch and ran its strong beam over each line of the writing. This was followed by another examination, this time by the reflected light of the table lamp. Swinburne watched anxiously. 'Do you see anything, Doctor?' he asked.

'I see no change of colour in any part of the paper, which is what I was looking for,' was the reply.

His next move was to take from his case a thin glass tube and pull forward one of the bottles of reagents which he had placed on the paper covering.

'What might that be, Doctor, and what is the object?' Mr. Swinburne put the question anxiously.

'In the bottle, do you mean? It is a five per cent solution of oxalic acid, and with it I propose to test some of the writing in this document.' He drew a little of the liquid from a bottle into the pipe — a pipette is the laboratory name for it — by compressing a small rubber bulb at the top of it — in the same way that a fountain-pen filler is filled with ink for transference into the barrel of the pen. He elaborated the experiment:

'When ordinary ink dries on paper, sir, it is slowly acted upon by the air, and gradually forms a resin-like substance which resists the action of all chemical reagents. Under normal conditions this change in the ink in writing takes about three years to complete . . . '

Alarm made itself visible on the face of the lawyer. 'But, Doctor, you surely do not intend to deface this document,' he protested. 'I may have to produce it to the owner.'

'Not at all, Mr. Swinburne, I assure you. There will be no defacement at all. I am proposing only to test the strokes of one or two of the letters; that will be sufficient, and it will not show to any disadvantage in the will. For instance, I inject a minute drop of the liquid on the downward stroke of the 'm' in the phrase 'my last will and testament'.' He did so, taking care that the drop was inferior to the width of the stroke. 'We will now wait and see what happens,' he announced.

After a moment or two he examined the treated stroke through his lens. 'There appears to be no reaction,' he announced. 'Very well, we will now repeat the operation on the word 'my' in the phrase 'To my niece, Aelthea Whiting I give and bequeath the sum of £5,000'.' He carefully placed a drop on the downward stroke of the tail of the 'y' and once more awaited any result. It did not appear to have any effect to the lawyer who, now assured of the safety of his document, was leaning forward watching eagerly the result of the tests.

For his third attempt Doctor Manson treated similarly the figure '5' in '5,000' placing the drop in the centre of the stroke, and again ensuring that the minute particle of liquid did not over-run the width of the stroke. Mr. Swinburne eyed it. Taking off his spectacles he rubbed the lenses and replaced them. 'Bless my soul,' he ejaculated, 'the figure appears to have grown fatter, or do my eyes deceive me.'

Doctor Manson had been peering at the figures and it was a moment or two before he answered. 'No, you are not deceived,' he said. 'There is a slight thickening, and a little uneven one, in the stroke.'

'Is there, Doctor?' The question came from Merry who had entered the library. He placed on the table a large porcelain dish containing an enlarged and still wet print of the photographed will. 'You have not tried the lower half of the will,' he added.

Together the pair treated in a similar

way the words towards the end of the document, which read: 'The residue of my estate I give and bequeath to my nephew, William Rawson, absolutely.'

Drops of the reagent were placed on the 't' in 'to', the 'p' in 'Nephew' and the 'A' in Aelthea Whiting and 'b' in 'absolutely'. Finally, the 'E' and the 'B' in the signature Eadwin Burstall were 'touched'. Once again there was only one blurring or running — in the letter 'p'.

The lawyer who had watched the experiments with interest, sat silent for a few moments. He appeared to be in deep thought. Then: 'Did you not say, Doctor Manson, that writing in ink after a certain lapse of time cannot be changed by a reagent?' he asked.

'I did say so, yes.'

'And did you not say, also, that the period of, shall I say incubation, was not less than three years?'

'That is the accepted time under normal conditions.'

'Do I infer that if a piece of writing is aged under the three it shows a reaction to chemical tests?' He waited in some anxiety for the answer. Doctor Manson eyed the will as he replied: 'Until the dried ink in writing has been thus acted upon by air and time, Mr. Swinburne, and has by that action formed its resin-like protection, it is inclined to run when touched by a reagent such as hydrochloric acid, sodium hydroxide or oxalic acid.'

Mr. Swinburne wiped his brow with a large yellow handkerchief which appeared with startling suddenness from an inside pocket of his morning coat. He looked appealingly at the scientist. 'I cannot help remarking, Doctor, that only three of the letters you tested showed any sign of change. Those letters in each instance appeared in those portions of the will in which the names of the legatees are mentioned. I am a lawyer used to assessing points of evidence, and it seems to me . . . ' His voice trailed off.

'The evidence, Mr. Swinburne, is undeniably in favour of the fact that this document' — he laid a hand on the will — 'was written not in its completeness at one time, but at two or more separate times, and at a lapse of some years between those times.'

'God bless me, that is a very serious thing to have happened. What do you suppose is the reason for that, sir?'

'There are, of course, various possible explanations. Mr. Burstall might tentatively have drawn up a will leaving the names of the recipients of his proposed bounty blank. And he may have filled them in later. It is odd that he should do such a thing, of course, but it could have happened.'

Mr. Swinburne considered again. 'If the document was indeed completed at different times that would not, of course, invalidate it as a testamentary document.' The lawyer threw the statement out as a challenge.

'I wonder,' Doctor Manson said. 'Can you as a lawyer think of any way in which the will could be invalidated through such an happening?'

The lawyer considered the point for some moments. Then he said, slowly: 'I can . . . see one way . . . in which the will

. . . could be rendered a useless document. And that is concerned with the date on which the witnesses attested their signatures.'

'I see,' Manson said. 'What would be the legal position if the signatories witnessed the will in its earlier stage, and that the benefits to Miss Whiting and William Rawson were added to the document subsequently?'

'Oh dear! oh dear!' Mr. Swinburne lapsed into depression. 'You do propound the most disturbing opinions. It might invalidate the whole will, though I don't think it would. I should have to have Counsel's opinion on that. There are, you remember, other benefits in the will, to the servants and Doctor Forrestal. If those could be shown to have been in the will when it was witnessed, those bequests would, I am sure, be legal. But legacies which were written in blank spaces at a later date and after the witnesses had recorded their names most certainly would not be lawfully distributable.'

'That is my own view of the position. The point may not arise. We may find that the witnesses attested the complete document. I suggest we may try.' He took up the will and placed it so that one of the tested letters came under the eyepiece of a microscope. He was about to look through the instrument when an idea came to him, and he addressed the lawyer again.

'Tell me, should it be found that your late client actually did fill in the names of the principal beneficiaries after the other parts of the will had been witnessed, and the will is invalidated in so far as those bequests are concerned, what would be the position in regard to the residue of the property?'

'It would go in equal proportions to the next of kin, sir, of course.'

'And who are they?'

'Bless me!' Mr. Swinburne sat up, startled. 'Why, they would be, of course, the nephew and niece.'

Doctor Manson smiled delightfully. 'So,' he said, 'this is becoming a problem after my heart. The £100,000 would be divided between William Rawson and Aelthea Whiting. Thus, instead of her

£5,000 legacy, Miss Whiting would receive the sum of £50,000 and Mr. Rawson a similar amount instead of the £100,000 left him under the will — less the amount of the other legacies of course.'

Mr. Swinburne looked up, a shocked expression on his face. 'Surely you are not suggesting — '

'I am not suggesting anything,' the Doctor retorted. 'I am merely stating facts.' He bent over the microscope and stared through it at a treated letter. He called to Merry: 'There is definite bleaching.' Merry noted the fact in his notebook. The will was then moved under the microscope until one of the treated strokes in the second set of letters — those of the names of the beneficiaries — came under the eyepiece. After a moment's pause, he beckoned Merry to the instrument. The Deputy Scientist examined the exhibit.

'Blue, I agree,' he announced.

'Do you know, Mr. Swinburne, whether your late client used any particular kind of ink, or inks?' Manson asked.

'I don't know . . . Perhaps Esther . . .'

The housekeeper, called in, was more helpful. 'The master had a big pot of ink, sir, from which he filled the inkwells in the house.' She vanished, to reappear with a stone bottle holding about a quart. Doctor Manson read the label descriptive of the contents, and examined a sample from it. A fourth note in the notebook was the result. Mr. Swinburne now completely mystified by the experiments, became a little restive. 'Where, Doctor, is this leading us?' he pleaded.

'We will tell you presently,' was the reply. 'Be patient. We have nearly reached the end of the road.' He placed rapidly under the microscope four parts of the photographic enlargements prepared by Merry. 'Did Mr. Burstall use a fountain pen?' he demanded.

'Never, sir.' The lawyer was emphatic on the point. 'He would use nothing but an ordinary Waverley nib.'

'I see.' Manson looked across at his companion. 'One thing would now, of course settle it. If we had ultra-violet rays . . .'

'I brought down a quartz lamp, Harry,' interrupted Merry. 'I thought we would most probably want to use that.' He left the room to return with the compact apparatus that Science has made available for harnessing the ultra-violet rays. It was switched on to the will of Eadwin Burstall. Plain to see, the paper on which the writing was recorded showed a violet or violet-blue fluorescence, except at two places. Those spaces appeared, instead, as dark stains which did not fluoresce.

The Doctor sat down for the first time; the examination was finished. 'Now, Mr. Swinburne,' he said.

'Ah! I hope by that you are satisfied at last as to the procedure followed by my late client,' he said.

'I am fully satisfied, Mr. Swinburne,' was the reply.

'Did my late client insert the names of the two principal beneficiaries after he had executed the main body of the document?'

'No, he did not.'

'Ah!' Mr. Swinburne rubbed his hands together in satisfaction. His seat in his chair visibly became more comfortable; he snuggled restfully into it in relaxation after the strain of waiting. The scientist regarded the action interestedly. The wrinkles had gone from the Manson brows, and the crinkles from his deepset eyes. But there was no relaxation in the poise of his tall form, no repose in the scholarly face; rather it displayed that vitality that comes from action of mind and vision. He looked hard at the lawyer and when he spoke it was with words that came slowly and very deliberately.

'I should advise you, Mr. Swinburne, to take the greatest possible care of this document,' he said, indicating the will. 'I advise you most earnestly to lock it away for the time being in your bank.'

He paused for a fraction before continuing. 'And I would further advise you at once to suspend any payments to anyone on the security of benefaction under the will. The late Mr. Burstall did not insert the names and legacies in the will after he had previously prepared the document. *He did not insert the names in the will at all. It is not, in fact, the last will* and *testament* of the late Eadwin Burstall.'

'Not the last will?' The lawyer stared at him. Incomprehension was written loudly on his face. 'Not the last will,' he stammered again. 'Then if it is not the late Mr. Burstall's will, what is it?'

Doctor Manson answered the question bluntly, in fact cruelly:

'There is no question at all as to what it is, Mr. Swinburne. *This will is a forgery.*'

9

Doctor Manson, Commander in the C.I.D., drove his car through the gateway of New Scotland Yard, and drew up in front of the C.I.D. entrance. He acknowledged the salute of the constable on duty.

'Is the A.C. in, Welsh?' he asked.

'Yes, sir. Arrived a few minutes ago.'

Manson nodded, walked up the stairs to the first floor and along a corridor. He stopped at a door, knocked and held it slightly open. 'Come,' said a voice, and Sir Edward Allen looked up.

'Harry!' He eyed his visitor in surprise. 'What the devil are you doing here. I thought I told you to be away for three months.'

'True, Edward. I've come to take you down to Cissing for a few days.'

'Then you pop off again. I haven't the time.'

Doctor Manson smiled. The smile had

a certain grimness about it. 'Never-the-less, Edward, I think you will return with me,' he said.

'Now, look, Harry. I've told you . . . ' His voice faded into silence and he looked sharply at his visitor. The two old cronies — as much in appreciation and understanding as in personal friendship. The 'I think you will return with me' aroused a certain suspicion and wariness in Sir Edward's mind. 'What have you been up to, Harry?' he demanded.

'Touché, Edward,' conceded the scientist. 'As a matter of fact I do not know. I know something, but I do not think I know it all. Listen to this . . . '

He sat down in one of the armchairs that grace the room of the Assistant Commissioner (C) of the Yard (the 'C' stands for crime), took a cigar from a case in his pocket, passed one over to the A.C., and with studied deliberation put a light to both of them.

'Now, Cissing, where you sent me, is the sleepiest country place. It has everything I crave for my leisure — fishing, golf, quietude almost unbelievable . . . '

'And the seed of trouble, apparently,' Sir Edward interrupted. 'Do I gather that you have been fertilizing the seed?'

'Unknowingly I have started it into a very troublesome growth.' Quietly, with conciseness that is born of an ordered and tidy brain, he painted the story of the library at 'Hengeclif', so that the picture of events was impasted on the canvas of the A.C.'s mind. He emphasised with jabs of his cigar the conclusions to which his probings, step by step, had driven him — to the *denouement* of the forgery.

'The *denouement* so far, Edward,' he ended. 'But I do not think it can be allowed to finish there. The trouble is that I have no standing down there. The matter ought, of course, to be reported to the local police. But I do not know any of them, and I feel that if any publicity gets about the place we may be hampered in the fuller investigation. In fact, I think the course of justice will be impeded. I thought you might be able to have a chat with the Chief Constable and see what steps we can take without the fact becoming generally known.'

Sir Edward surveyed his scientist investigator through his monocle. 'I don't wonder you cannot find peace and quietness, Harry,' he said. 'With a mind like yours you wouldn't find peace and quietness in the Celestial Regions. If you had given the derned place a holiday, which is what you were told to do, we wouldn't have been in this unholy mess. Nevertheless, I'll come down with you. Where's Merry?'

'Keeping watch and ward over the exhibits and events in regard to any possible visitors.'

The county town of West Sussex is Chichester, the *Cissa's Ceaster* of the Saxons. The Chief Constable there, appraised by telephone of the desire of the Assistant Commisioner of Scotland Yard to see him on an urgent private matter, awaited them, a tall soldierly figure, straight-backed as befitted a former officer of the Guards despite his sixty years. 'Pleased to meet you, Doctor,' he greeted Manson. 'Know all about you, of course. You proved a man of mine wrong in one case, I remember. Hope this visit doesn't mean trouble.'

'Afraid it does, Captain,' the A.C. answered, 'but perhaps Doctor Manson had better tell the story as he has told it to me.'

Once again the scientist recounted the processes of thought and chemistry which led to his certainty that the will was a forgery; and demonstrated the experiments with the inked letters of the will, allied to the fact that no reagent will affect the strokes of letters written in ink after such letters are three years old; and emphasised the fact that a drop of oxalic acid will cause ink to run if the words were written under three years. 'You have seen the results of the reaction in the thickened letters of the names of the two principal legatees in the will,' he said.

'Now, an important point of any investigation is concerned with the suggestion that Mr. Burstall had previously prepared the body of the will, and later filled in the names,' he went on. 'We must consider that possibility.' He edged a portion of the photographed enlargement of the will under his microscope. 'If you will look at this,' he urged, 'you will see along the outside of each of the letters in turn the scratches made by the divided points of a steel pen as the letters were written.'

The Chief Constable nodded. 'Quite plainly,' he admitted.

'Now will you examine that part of the will which gives the names of the legatees.' He adjusted the microscope.

'There are no marks,' the Chief Constable said.

'Now, the only pen that could thus write and leave no such scratches, sir, is a pen having a golden nib — in other words a fountain pen. Mr. Burstall did not use a fountain pen. He had never used one, and did not possess one.'

The Chief Constable clapped his hands. 'This, Doctor Manson, looks like magic,' he said. 'Could you, do you think, prove that Shakespeare did not write his plays by an inspection of manuscripts?' The Chief Constable was the president of the local Baconian Society.

'Probably, if you could present me with a MS which you could assure me was Shakespeare's and one which was Bacon's. The final point I want to make concerns the very enlightening revelations from an inspection of the will under ultra-violet rays. Under the quartz lamp, he pointed out the bluish fluorescence thrown up by the will as a whole with the exception of the darkened portions which bore the names and amounts of the benefactors under the will. He answered the enquiring look of the Chief Constable:

'All writing paper has sized surfaces. In ultra-violet light this sized surface shows the bluish fluorescence you have seen. But where that sized surface has been removed either by erasure or by chemical action, then it does not fluoresce, but shows up as a dark, unlightened stain. *Therefore I say that this will has been altered by having certain portions of it washed out with chemicals — under a powerful lens you can see the slight yellow staining left by the washing out though it is not apparent to the unaided eyesight, so skifully has it been done — and other wording has been written in the imitated handwriting of the supposed testator.*

'Since there would be no sense in the testator himself going to all that trouble and industry, I can only arrive at the belief that the inserted words which we now see are forgeries in the simulated handwriting of the late Eadwin Burstall.'

'Who by?' the Chief Constable asked.

'As to that I have no evidence of any kind, and I do not deal in theories unsupported by facts.'

Sir Edward Allen sat silent during the arguments. He had been swinging his monocle by its ribbon, a sure sign that there was something he did not understand. He now broke into the conversation:

'Why, Doctor, should the forger go to all this trouble of erasing names and bequests from the will to insert other names when he could have forged an entirely new will without all that trouble. The writing was accepted by Mr. Swinburne as that of a dead client and friend?'

'As I see it, Sir Edward, the answer is simple. It is much easier and safer to forge the writing in a dozen words and get it passed unnoticed than it would be to create an absolutely new deed. *Furthermore, there can be no doubting at all that the signature on the will is that of Eadwin Burstall, and the forger knew that it would pass all tests.* Thirdly, he could have no opportunity of getting a sample of the writing of the witnesses, which he would have to forge.'

The Chief Constable started in sudden surprise. The scientist's argument had opened up a hitherto ignored point in the story.

'Signatures, witnesses, Doctor?' he asked. 'How did they get on the document in the first place? Where did they come from?'

Doctor Manson laughed, though there was no humour in the sound. It was more the laugh of a man who had been keeping something under his hat, and had now seen that the time had come to pull it out. 'I was wondering when someone was going to ask me that,' he said.

'*The answer, I think, is that this will is the original will, the one under which Rawson was a co-partner in the residue.*

It was never, as was thought, destroyed. That is, of course, an answer to the discoloured envelope despite the fact that the will is supposed to be only a few months old. All that was necessary was to change, also, the date of the will from seven years or more ago to the present date, and alter the wording of a couple of lines, and you had what by the ordinary tests was a perfectly good document, the signatures on which could be attested by any handwriting expert. In fact, it was so tested by an expert employed by Mr. Swinburne, who merely checked on the signatures. It was a thousand to one against' — and the forger knew it — 'that any expert would alight out of the mass of material in the will on those two lines after he had assured himself as to the authenticity of the signatures.'

'True.' The Chief Constable looked at his guests.

'And, of course, you want me to get busy and find the forger, it being outside the area of Scotland Yard?'

The A.C. was about to speak when Doctor Manson interrupted sharply. 'No,

Chief Constable, that is not the idea at all,' he said abruptly. 'The reason for our visit is that we do not want you to do anything openly in the forgery for the moment. There is another, and much more important aspect of the matter. I am not so interested in the forgery of the will as I am interested in the reason for the forgery.' He paused, and gravity crept into his voice.

'What I do not know, and what I want to know, is whether this forged will was a means to a quick end. *I want to know whether, to bring this forged will into operation, old man Burstall was murdered.*'

10

'Murdered!'

The cry came from the Chief Constable. It wailed out almost despairingly in articulate protest that murder and the Chichester diocese should be so promiscuously commingled even in mind, let alone in thought.

Doctor Manson repeated the word: 'Murder I said, and murder I repeat,' he insisted. 'Mind you,' he added hastily, 'I did not make a *pronunciamento* that murder *has* been done; I said I wanted to know *whether* Eadwin Burstall had been murdered.'

'*Ante tubum trepidat,*' said the A.C., who had a penchant for speaking the Latin tongue when he could remember in time the apt words. He was enjoying the interview, and his reason for suggesting that the Doctor's courage was oozing before the ferocity of the Chief Constable defending his law-abiding flock was merely to propel him still closer into the fray.

'The two sound synonymous to me,' retorted the Chief Constable. 'You have suggested that Eadwin Burstall was murdered — all right, *may* have been murdered,' he added, hastily, as Doctor Manson prepared to interrupt. 'What grounds have you for considering such a crime?'

'What I suppose Mr. Wills would call Circumstantial Evidence, sir. I, personally, call it logical deduction. You will remember that Cuvier from a single fossil bone was able, because of his profound knowledge of comparative anatomy, to describe the structure and habits of many extinct animals of the antediluvian world.'

The Chief Constable, who had never heard of Cuvier, looked a little distraught at the news.

'And the perturbations of Uranus led astronomers by a process of inference to believe in the existence of a planet outside the then Solar system long before the place of Neptune was discovered.' He paused as though for comment. None was forthcoming, but the A.C. gained the impression that the Chief Constable at the moment would have been satisfied had he possessed the three-pronged trident of the *other* Neptune.

'In like manner,' the scientist went on, 'an enlightened knowledge of human nature often enables us on the foundations of apparently slight circumstances to follow the tortuous windings of crime, and ultimately to discover the guilty author as infallibly as the hunter is conducted by the track to his game.

'Now we have here, sir, a will altered, and certain substantial benefits inserted in it. The author of this deed put in a very considerable amount of time and skill, and he or she used a great deal of knowledge on inks and how to colour them so that they would match old ink on a document. I therefore asked myself to what purpose was all this labour and care lavished on the document. There is, of course, only one answer — for personal gain by somebody. *But the gain can only accrue if the testator, or alleged testator, departs this life.*

'Thus, when the supposed testator does, *ipso facto*, depart this life, and that within a few weeks of the forgery, and the forged bequests in the will become operative, I ask myself whether this shuffling off this mortal coil was not helped prematurely by the aid of a healthy push. *What would you think?*'

'Um!' The Chief Constable conceded the point, but grudgingly. 'Put that way, it does seem suspicious. Of course it may be coincidence. Burstall was an old man.'

'Of whom Doctor Forrestal had said a few days previously that there was no likelihood of him dying. Yet a few days later he is dead. There is another indicatory pointer which seems also to autograph murder . . . '

'This is where something is going to come out of the hat,' the A.C. whispered to Merry.

Doctor Manson produced a packet from his case and, taking from it three separate slips of paper laid them on the desk. They were the three slips of paper on which had been written the notes on poison. 'Three people have been playing

'Hunt the Slipper' in my library,' he explained. 'These prying inquisitors developed so keen a desire to possess some object contained in the shelves that Chief Inspector Merry and I thought it convenient to join their ranks.' He described the search through the volumes of the library. 'These are what we found,' he said.

'Um!' commented the Chief Constable. He seemed to have a particular affection for the monosyllable. 'What did Burstall die of?'

'I do not know. But it was obviously something to do with the heart.'

'We can soon get to know from Doctor Forrestal,' the Chief said, and reached for the phone.

'Forrestal was one of the seekers,' intimated Doctor Manson.

'The Devil,' ejaculated the Chief, and replaced the receiver.

'Forrestal got a nice little sum out of the will,' the A.C. said, 'and, of course, opportunity to obtain poison.'

'But, damn it, the man's well off,' protested the Chief. 'He's worth at least

£20,000 himself.'

'And he wouldn't want any notes on poison,' Manson put in. 'He knows all about them. As a matter of fact, he has an excellent library on poisons. I've looked through them. The books are unmarked.'

'You said just now, Doctor, that you did not know from what Burstall died but expected it was something to do with the heart. Why the heart?' The Chief Constable put the question.

'Because all the poisons to which reference is made in these slips of paper possess one characteristic in common — dispensed to a person they would lead to a deterioration in the pressure of the blood and the respiratory organs.'

'How would anyone get hold of these poisons?'

'As concerns the Aconite,' the A.C. put in, 'you just dig up some roots of Monkshood — there'll be plenty in the fields round here. Then you dry the roots and powder them. I read that in a detective story,' he added.

At this point the Chief Constable came

to the realisation that they were discussing a serious crime problem in his area. 'Ought I not to call in my superintendent and a chief inspector?' he asked.

The Assistant Commissioner fixed his monocle in his perfectly good left eye, and spoke. 'That, C.C. is why we came to see you,' he said. 'We would, in ordinary circumstances, hand over the case to you. But we feel . . . that there are certain peculiarities here which may call for different action. We do not know whether Mr. Burstall was killed for his fortune, and we do not know who forged the will. If inquiries became public property I think our task will be almost impossible. One of the persons is now abroad in a place from where, if he cares to stay, he cannot be extradited. Inquiries by members of your force would be public within a very short space of time; not only are your men known, but it is obvious that any questions they asked would be easily recognisable as having a local interest.

'On the other hand, if inquiries were, as it were, casually made by Scotland Yard officers who would be strangers here, and in the place as holidaymakers, I feel we could complete inquiries without arousing suspicion. When the case came to a successful conclusion, then we would hand it over to you. It properly belongs to you.'

'It seems an unwarranted interference with the rights of the local C.I.D., Mr. Assistant Commissioner,' the C.C. said.

'Then, Chief, say no more about it,' Sir Edward apologised. 'We will forget it.'

The Chief Constable held up a hand. 'I was about to say, sir, that I think with you that the course of justice may well be impeded if we hold to our rights of investigation. It will be agreed, of course, that our action is not to be regarded as a precedent?'

'Of course. Then I take it that nothing of which we have talked here will be revealed outside this room?'

'Agreed.'

The next moves in the case were discussed in 'Hengeclif' after luncheon. The A.C. turned to the forgery side of the problem. 'Assuming for the sake of argument, Harry, that Burstall did for

145

once use a fountain pen, to fill in the names of the nephew and niece, would that in any way negative your views?'

'It would not. The inks in the will are perfectly matched, despite the evidence, scientifically manifestable, that they are of widely separated periods. It demonstrates that whatever pen was used the ink must have been treated over a period of time in order to obtain the colour.'

'How would he — or she — get the colour?' Sir Edward put the question.

'I cannot say. Expose it to the air over a time, or something like that. Or treat it with coffee. What does it matter? The second point is that the only ink Burstall had in the house is a black gallotanic. That is proved by the reagent test showing a little bleaching. But the ink used by the forger under the same reagent showed no bleaching but a definite blue colour . . . '

'Meaning that it was *blue*-black gallo-tanic ink, of course,' Merry said. 'Who is the forger?'

'Obviously the murderer,' answered Sir Edward.

'I have never prognosticated that,' Doctor Manson protested. 'I have said that murder may have followed the forgery because, to my mind, that is, on the facts we have in front of us, the only logical procedure. But that does not mean, necessarily, that the forger was the murderer.'

'What do you mean by that?' The A.C. looked in bewilderment.

'Well, the obvious candidate for arrest as the forger is the nephew. He inherits all the estate with the exception of about £6,000 or so instead, as hitherto, being disinherited in favour of his lady cousin. Even in the old will, we are informed, that the estate was evenly divided between the two cousins.'

'Admitted,' said the A.C.

'But there is no evidence at all that the nephew Rawson has the slightest connection with this list of poisons. Miss Whiting searched for it — if we are correct in assuming that the list is that for which she was looking. Esther searched for it. And Doctor Forrestal seems to have had a good look round for something. Neither

Esther nor Forrestal have a good word to say for Rawson; in fact they hate his guts. So I cannot see them helping him to get rid of anything by assisting him to search for it. In fact, they would have been glad to give him away. Both Forrestal and Esther are close friends of Miss Whiting.'

'Harry! ... You don't mean' — Sir Edward became very plaintive — 'you don't mean that TWO people were trying to polish off the old man?'

11

'As to whether there are, or not, two people with but a single thought of murder I cannot say, Edward,' Doctor Manson replied to the A.C.'s question. 'We would seem to have rather an *embarras de richesse*.'

'In whose handwriting are the poison notes? Anything to be gained there?'

'I do not know. It could be a man's calligraphy, or it could equally be that of a woman. We cannot inquire in the house as to whose writing it resembles. I gather that Forrestal has no writing at all of Rawson. There was none in the papers in the desk.'

'It seems to be,' the A.C. said, 'that the actions of the people in our minds do not co-ordinate into a truthful entity. If they did we would have the answer to who killed the man.'

'This is getting a little out of my depth,' Manson protested. 'What exactly do you mean by that?'

'It seems to me to announce itself as fairly axiomatic. The only person who can benefit under the forged will is the nephew — *ergo*, he must be the forger. The only person to lose under the will is Miss Whiting, who drops some £45,000 or more.'

'Agreed.'

'Now, since the nephew benefits, he is the most likely candidate for ending the old man's life. Yet the facts are that there is nothing of a suspicious nature connected with the nephew so far as murder goes — nothing concretely connected with actual murder, that is — whereas the niece is believed to be searching frantically, with the aid of her friends, for a book in which has been hidden notes on poison and their effect on anyone to whom they may be administered. That is what I meant when I said the facts do not co-ordinate. Would she commit murder to lose money?'

Doctor Manson countered the question with one of his own. '*Would she commit murder for nearly £100,000?*' he asked.

The A.C. grinned. 'I'd nearly commit

murder myself for that sum,' he retorted. 'Seriously, though, I should say that the temptation to do so would want a little fighting down, if she was at all that way inclined.'

'Well, my dear Edward, that is the sum at stake if she was playing murder. *Because, you see, she did not know of the existence of the altered will. Under the old will, of which she had cognisance, she was the residue heiress.* That is the point that is causing considerable lucubrationary activities in the back of my head.'

'Heaven call vengence on your head for your suspicions of her,' the A.C. said. 'She had been the residue heiress for three years, since the nephew had been kicked out, and despite the fact that her life appears to have been more or less confinement in a luxury prison she had tended her uncle with loving care. All that time there is no suspicion that she wanted to get rid of him. Now you want suddenly to imbue her gentle breast with murderous intent. Why?'

Doctor Manson stared at the A.C. with sombre eyes. 'You fail to make allowances for the Biblical dictum that the old order changeth,' he said. 'It is true that for years she attended her uncle without showing any evidence that she was developing into a consanguineous Septembrist, so to speak. She had no inducement and there was no inducement to murder. *She was the heiress to old Eadwin Burstall.*

'But now mark the changed circumstances. Suddenly the prodigal nephew returns to the avuncular fold; the profligate who was kicked off the premises and disinherited reappears, and in good odour.'

'With a consequent lessening of Miss Whiting's hereditous prospects — yes, I see the point,' the A.C. admitted.

'So. Let us surmise a little further in that direction,' Manson went on. 'The lady realises that *le pot au lait* is likely to spill an appreciable amount of its cream. But she also realises that there is no visit, so far, from Mr. Swinburne. If that means anything to her it is that Uncle Eadwin's will, yet, as she knows in the hands of the lawyer, is still functioning. But probably not for long.

There, my dear Edward, there is the stimulus, the incitement to murder . . . while the money is good.'

'And then, after the man's death we find her searching for a list of poisons,' said the A.C. reflectively.

'On the other hand,' interrupted Manson, 'the same arguments can be adumbrated of the nephew. He is back in favour, but not so much in favour, it seems, as to have persuaded uncle to send for the lawyer and alter the will. So he — presumably — forges a document abrogating uncle's dalliance. Thereafter he *must* kill so that the will becomes effective.'

'And he has to do it fairly quickly,' Merry emphasised. 'Because if he has a date on the forged will he cannot chance waiting long enough for uncle to decide on cancelling the old will and making still another, for the date of that would post-date his own forgery and make it null and void.'

Sir Edward worked it out. 'The inference is that he must have decided to murder before he forged the will, and was

153

in all probability even then effecting the murder.'

'And we've no idea how,' Merry said.

'Or even if!' Doctor Manson waxed sarcastic. 'And if we keep talking we never will. I'm going to see Sir Charles Hurley and have a check-up,' he announced. He winked at the A.C. 'Hurley, what's he got to do with it?' Sir Edward asked.

'Burstall was his specialist patient.'

★ ★ ★

The specialist ran the rule over him. 'Fifty per cent improvement, Doctor,' he announced. 'You see what rest and a mind kept free from dwelling on crime can do. Like the place, eh?'

'Ideal. I've Eadwin Burstall's excellent library to go at, and his quiet garden to sit in. Patient of yours, wasn't he?'

Sir Charles nodded. 'Forrestal called me in towards the end. Thought he shouldn't have gone down so quickly . . . '

'And you polished him off! Did you examine him yourself?'

'Yes. After reading through Forrestal's

history of the case. The usual thing in old people — low blood pressure, laboured breathing. He was in a semi-coma when I saw him.'

'Was there any sickness or diarrhoea mentioned by Forrestal?'

'Not to my remembrance. I . . . ' Sir Charles took a sharp look at the scientist. 'Why this remarkable interest in the life and death of Eadwin Burstall? Is his ghost playing Hamlet with you in his old library?'

'Something like that.' Manson evaded the glance, looking intently at the cigarette he was twisting in his fingers. '*And crying out for vengeance, I think,*' he added.

Sir Charles looked at him curiously. 'You aren't . . . '

'Gone out of my mind?' Manson finished the question for him. 'No, I am still in possession of my senses.' He took from his pocket the list of poisons, placed it on the table and covered it with a hand. 'If you remember that old Burstall's eyes were closed he being in a semi-coma, and add to the blood pressure and depressed aspiration a certain amount of sickness and diarrhoea, Charles, which of these would the symptoms fit?' His hand moved and exposed the list.

Sir Charles glanced at it. 'Great Scott, man! Are you trying to tell me he was poisoned?' he burst out.

'I am not trying to tell you anything, Charles. I asked which of these symptoms would fit?'

'All of them more or less.' He read slowly through the list. 'Probably Benzaconine and Venatrine would be the nearest.'

'That is precisely my own opinion,' agreed Manson. He picked up his hat and stick, bade Charles Hurley good-bye, and left.

The specialist stared at the closed door and puckered his lips.. 'What the devil is he up to?' he asked without expecting any answer.

Merry motored down to Cissing that evening, and telephoned back to his chief the following morning. 'Back me up, Doctor,' he said. 'On the plea that Forrestal had asked us to send Miss

Whiting a packet she had been promised, but that we had forgotten the number of the street, I persuaded Esther to give it to me, after she said she knew it.' Manson noted down the address and sent for Detective Superintendent Jones, Old Fat Man of the Yard, whose baby-like face and innocent guile could extract blood out of a stone and statements out of the most alert-minded crook.

'Have a talk with her, Fat Man,' he said, 'and in some way induce her to handle something you can bring away. We want her prints.'

The telephone call from Merry had been taken by the doctor in his laboratory while he was engaged in laying out various apparatus on his porcelain covered bench. One such piece had the appearance of a small clothes wringer similar to that used by housewives screwed to the board of a washing machine. Another was a half-plate camera and easel, the latter lighted by photo-flood lamps.

From a bottle he emptied a little of the contents into a dish, and with a soft brush moistened the rollers of the wringer with a film of the liquid. He then inserted one of the sheets of the poison list found in the library at 'Hengeclif' in the roller, and propelled it through the machine, taking it out at the back.

'Regular old washerwoman you'd make, Harry,' said the A.C., who sat by watching the experiments.

'A washerwoman wouldn't be very pleased with the result, Edward. You see, we wash dirt on to the material instead of out of it. Watch.'

The processed paper was fixed under the hot breath of a drier. When satisfied that it was bone dry, the scientist played over the surface, front and back, with the rays of an ultra-violet lamp. Over the surfaces of the paper there appeared a number of black smudges which gradually revealed themselves as fingerprints.

'What did you use?' the A.C. asked.

'Nitrate of silver.' He passed the sheet over to Wilkins the Laboratory Chief Assistant, who pinned it on the easel and switched on the camera floodlight. A moment later he took from the camera the slide containing the exposed plate and went away with it for development.

'But — have I not read that nitrate of silver prints are permanent, Harry,' the A.C. asked. 'Why photograph them as well?'

'They are, but only if kept in the dark. They can be fixed, but it's a chancy business, and if it fails then the prints cannot be brought up on the paper again. So a photograph is good evidence, provided that we can prove it's genuine. And you can do that — which is why you are here at all. We now have to wait a while.' He lit a cigarette.

The laboratory door opened, and the sixteen-stone figure of Superintendent Jones appeared panting in the doorway. His eyes fell on Sir Edward. 'Gawd's truth, A.C . . . wish . . . you'd . . . put lift here . . . Be . . . death . . . of me . . . these stairs.' He caught sight of Doctor Manson. 'Cor . . . Old Trouble . . . still . . . here . . . No ruddy peace at all.' The words came in staccato bursts, like intermittent machine-gun fire. Jones always talked like that. He was built that way, talking what the Yard men called shorthand.

Manson laughed. 'Still groaning, I see,' he said. 'Sit down and tell us why you come winging up here like Mercury.'

'Mercury?' Jones turned a suspicious eye on the scientist. 'Who's 'e?'

'Well, Icarus, perhaps.'

'Icar . . . '

The A.C. wiped tears of mirth from his eyes. 'Never mind him, Fat Man,' he urged. 'Icarus was a gentleman who made himself a pair of wings a few thousand years ago, and flew and fell. You can't be him. You'd want a couple of aeroplanes. What has heaved you up to this abode of magic?'

The fat superintendent turned his gaze on Manson. 'Your bird . . . name Whiting . . . '

'Yes?' queried Manson.

'Well . . . she ain't . . . name Brandon . . . see . . . Got married.'

'I'm not dumbfounded, Fat Man. I knew she was getting married.'

'Ho! Bird . . . flown.'

'What!' Manson started in surprise. 'Flown where?'

"'Merica . . . in plane.' Jones chuckled. 'Bird flown . . . really flown.'

Manson and A.C. exchanged glances. 'Has she given up the flat?' the Doctor asked.

'Week ago . . . tried tie-up with flat. No good.'

'Why not?'

'Furnished flat . . . let again . . . walls washed down . . . redecorating . . . no chance prints.'

'Damn,' the A.C. said. 'What are we going to do now?'

'There's just one chance. If she's gone to America, then the embassy have her fingerprints.'

'What the devil for?' asked the astonished A.C.

'I don't know. But you can take it they are on her visa. Every applicant for a visa to enter America has on the appropriate form each of the fingers of each hand imprinted separately, and then all five pressings of each hand. Now, if we can persuade the Embassy officials to let us have the prints for a few minutes . . . '

'I'll have a try — through the Commissioner,' the A.C. said, and went out of the room.

A minute or two later the laboratory door opened to admit Inspector Thompson, head of the fingerprint department. He carried the photographic copies of the poison lists with him.

'Any luck?' Manson asked.

'A little, Doctor. There are prints of two characters well known to us. We can pull them in any time . . . '

'The deuce there are. Who?'

'Couple who work always in partnership — name of Manson and Merry.' He dodged a probing finger of the scientist. 'Seriously, however,' he said, 'there are a dozen or so overlaid prints, of which we have no records because overlaying has smudged them. But there are two prints on the surface of the top page and three on the underside of the third of the three pages.' He indicated them.

'As though the fingers had held the sheets while they were pinned together. Do I gather you know them?'

'Yes, they belong to Black Timmins. We've had him inside on several occasions.'

'The devil,' Manson, shocked, said. He was about to speak further when the A.C. returned. 'The Embassy will not let us have the prints, but we can send a man over to check them,' he announced. He saw the Prints chief. 'Thompson any help to us?'

'He might be.' Doctor Manson repeated the inspector's report. 'Black Timmins? What is he? A coloured man?'

'No sir. The name is a nickname because Timmins is known to us as a blackmailer.'

'Man about town,' Jones broke in. 'Dapper . . . charmin' . . . Ingrat — ingrat — what do you call it?'

'Ingratiates himself, do you mean?' the A.C. suggested.

'That's it . . . ingr . . . what you say . . . with 'em. Gets 'em in compromising position . . . blackmail's 'em.'

'Oh!' Doctor Manson scratched his head. 'Doesn't sound much like Miss Whiting, but . . . ' He turned to

Thompson. 'Can you dash over to the U.S. Embassy, visa department.' He explained to the prints chief the problem they had to solve. 'Better take one of our lists and prints to check from. The name may be either Whiting or Brandon. We don't know whether the visa is in her single or married name.'

'This begins to look nasty, Harry,' the A.C. said. 'Was this Whiting girl a bit of a go-er?'

'I shouldn't have thought so. Seemed by all reports to be a stay-at-home woman. She had no followers down there and the household, even Doctor Forrestal, were staggered to know that she was even thinking of getting married. We'll have to . . .'

The telephone shrilled. Doctor Manson lifted the receiver. 'Your Cissing call, sir,' said the operator. 'You're through.' A voice called, 'Swinburne here. Who are you?'

'This is Manson, in London. Tell me, have you paid Miss Whiting any money on account of her legacy under the Burstall will?'

There was a pause and the muted sound of a voice sounded in the laboratory. 'How much?' Manson asked. 'I see. Thanks very much. Swinburne has paid out £5,000 to her on her IOU and authority to transfer the sum from the estate when probate is obtained,' he said.

'Then I should think we know what the answer from Thompson will be,' the A.C. said. 'I don't like the look of things at all. One of the pair in Monte Carlo where we won't be able to touch him, and the other in the USA where she can pop down into South America and we won't be able to get her back either.'

'It looks that way, Edward,' agreed Manson.

Inspector Thompson returned a quarter-of-an-hour later. 'Visa in the name of Brandon, Doctor,' he said. 'Prints in our photograph are those of her left thumb and two fingers of that hand, and four of the thumb of her right hand.'

'That settles it, Doctor,' said the Assistant Commissioner.

12

Doctor Manson and the Assistant Commissioner were two at a conference of five in Sir Edward Allen's room at Scotland Yard next morning. The other three were Superintendent Jones, Chief Inspector Kenway and Mr. Horace Abigail, the Home Office expert.

Mr. Abigail ('Stiffy' to the Yard) was a meek little man with a bulging forehead placed some five feet four inches from the ground and thatched with a rapidly failing thatch of red hair. His eyes protruded, and this fact with the addition of a long, thin nose gave him a somewhat comical appearance not at all in keeping with his melancholy expression; it was a moot point with the Home Office and Scotland Yard staffs whether his lugubrity was due to nature of his pathological calling, or to a permanent revolt against his personal appearance. But whatever his outward and visible form 'Stiffy' Abigail was hosannahed on all hands as an authority of considerable note on dead bodies.

He listened to the Strange Affair of the Library at 'Hengeclif' and the subsequent developments that had come from the Yard laboratory. 'Now, Mr. Abigail,' the A.C. had concluded, 'Doctor Manson thinks your advice should be sought.' He sat back awaiting the expert's *res judicata*.

Flattered by the Yard's confidence in his judgement, Mr. Abigail surveyed the company through the pince-nez perched at the end of his long nose, and then removed his glasses, laying them on the arm of his armchair. 'It assumes in my eyes a very sinister appearance,' he began in his usual pedantic language. 'I do think that the interests of Justice can be served only by making sure of the nature of the final illness and death of the defunct Mr. Burstall.'

He looked from the A.C. to the Doctor and received from each an approving nod. 'That means, of course, an exhumation,' he went on. 'A very grave undertaking.'

'Very grave indeed,' admitted the A.C. solemnly, but his eyes twinkled. Stiffy did not see the pun.

'And one which the Home Secretary is very loth to authorise except in very exceptional circumstances. Viewing the manner of death and the list of poisons, Sir Charles Hurley's and Doctor Manson's explanation of the circumstances, and of the symptoms said to have been exhibited in the illness of the deceased, and the fact that the niece's fingerprints are on the same list of poisons as those of a well-known criminal, I feel justified in counselling the Minister of the desirability of the exhumation of the corpse.'

Sir Edward thanked him, whereupon Mr. Abigail left the room.

The remaining three next turned to the police aspect of the case. 'Now, what are we going to do next, Doctor?' the A.C. asked. 'There are, for instance the prints of Timmins. Any idea where he is, Jones?'

'He's . . . about . . . the place. Saw . . . him . . . 'self . . . week ago. Can . . . pick . . . up . . . any time.'

Doctor Manson interposed. 'Not yet,

168

Fat Man.' he said. 'Let's get some line on him first. He is not going to acknowledge the acquaintance, so the more we know of him and the Whiting woman the better. You and Kenway may be able to find some loose threads in Brunswick Terrace where her flat was. She must be known by someone round there. She had to buy food, and the commissionaire and servants in the flat must know something about her. I don't suppose that 'Black' will run away for a few days. Meantime, I will see what can be done in Cissing.'

He and Merry went down the same afternoon. The scientist's efforts there opened with an attempt to startle Esther into what might be termed guilty knowledge. 'I suppose you know that Miss Whiting is married, Esther?' he said.

The woman looked at him in astonishment. 'Married, Miss Aelthea, sir.' There's no doubt of her surprise, Manson decided for himself. 'Lawks sir, when did that happen?'

'I should say a day or two ago, in London.'

'And me never asked to the wedding. I

never heard the likes of it. Why, us never knew she was courting. Would it be anyone we know?'

'Couldn't say, Esther. I gather it was a Mr. Brandon.'

'Never heard of a Brandon. My, that dratted girl did know something after all.'

Doctor Manson looked at her sharply. 'What dratted girl, Esther?' he asked.

'That Daphne Crooks, sir. When they were a'burying of poor Mr. Burstall and we was cooking lunch for the mourners and saying that we might have a bit of youth in the place now that Miss Aelthea was mistress, Daphne said as she might be getting married. When we said that Miss had no interest in men she said as how she knew what she knew. I suppose she'd been rummaging among Miss Aelthea's letters, seeing that she used to look after her things for her.'

When, an hour later, the girl served after dinner coffee in the library, 'How did you know, Daphne, that Miss Whiting was thinking of being married?' Manson asked her. The girl showed signs of confusion, and made no immediate response. 'There is nothing to be frightened about, Daphne,' the Doctor said. 'Most lady's maids have good knowledge of their mistress's little affairs, you know. They see things and hear things. And they very often act as go-betweens.' The girl reacted.

'Well, sir,' she said, 'I didn't actually *know*. I only guessed. I knew she had a boy-friend and most girls get married when they have young gentlemen.'

'It seems a reasonable assumption, and, of course you had seen some of the letters.'

The girl coloured again. 'Well, I did see one or two when I was clearing up after her. And I used to post letters for her addressed to him.'

'Of course. That would be to the Royal Hotel, Eastbourne, eh?'

'Oh, no sir. It was to the Louvre Hotel at Brighton, where Miss Aelthea stayed for a week once on holiday.'

'I suppose you never saw Mr. Brandon?'

'No, sir. I don't think he ever came here . . . ' She hesitated and wrinkled her brows. 'Who did you say, sir?' she asked.

'I said Mr. Brandon. Miss Whiting is now Mrs. Brandon. You say he never visited here?'

'No, sir. But that wasn't the name. It was Mr. Fortesque who wrote to Miss Aelthea.'

Doctor Manson looked at her in surprise. 'Fortesque — are you sure?' he demanded.

'Quite sure, sir. It was the same name as a boy-friend I had at the time, and I thought it was odd that we both had a Fortesque. I used to post letters to my friend at the same time I posted Miss Aelthea's.'

'We progress, Jim,' he said to Merry after the girl had gone. 'There appears now to be three men in Miss Whiting's life, of whom one is, we know a professional blackmailer. A trip to Brighton seems desirable.'

He left the room for a moment, to reappear with a framed photograph that had been hanging on the wall of the dining-room. The face on it was that of Aelthea Whiting. 'Better copy this with the camera, I think, Jim. Get a couple of large prints for ourselves, and then send the negative to Scotland Yard.'

★   ★   ★

If you take the long straight road outside the railway station at Brighton and walk to the end, you come to the sea almost at the point where the Palace Pier juts out for a quarter of a mile. If, then, you turn left a road runs upwards in a steep slope. It climbs and drops, and climbs and drops again on its straight path over the Downs — over the ups and downs would be a better description — but never is it out of the sight of the sea moving bluely restless in summer, and greyishly angry in winter; and the wind sweeps over its surface and, laden with ozone, over the land to the houses which stand arrogantly against it, whether it be zephyr softness, or comes to them in screaming fury.

Over those Downs the Saxons wandered, and the Romans. William the Norman handed three parcels of land there to his captain, William de Warenne, who exacted toll from the fisherfolk who were the dwellers. He sold a parcel of land to Earl Godwin, and the fishers then had to pay a yearly rental of four thousand herrings on behalf of the community.

The Saxons have gone, and the Romans have gone, and so have the Earls Godwin; and the rent is no longer in herrings, but in paper money. In place of the Norman visitors bent on extracting dues, holidaymakers now visit the town, and topsy-turvily the residents have reversed the Norman custom — *they* now exact dues from the *visitors*; it costs sixpence to sit on a deckchair on the sea front.

Way up on these Downs, on the first plateau above Brighton, there sits the cluster of habitations known as Rottingdean. It stands high above the sea, on the very edge of the cliffs in the face of which ravens nest in holes in their hundreds. And if you stand in the square formed by the meeting of four crossroads and follow your nose for a hundred yards or so you will pass the house which announces by plaque that Burne Jones, the painter of pictures, lived there (whereas he didn't but had his habitation in Fulham in London, though he paid occasional visits to Rottingdean) and arrive eventually at the Louvre Hotel. It was to the hotel that the two Yard officers had wended a way in search of the second instalment of the story of Miss Whiting.

It is understandable that the manager did not see eye to eye with them; hotels do not take kindly to inquiries by police officers however exalted their rank; in fact the higher the rank the more serious the trouble invariably is. It was only when he was assured that his *khan* was not concerned with their seeking, but that his inquisitors were only interested in searching for a lost lady, that he expressed himself as willing to assist.

Search of the register brought no news of any visitor named Whiting. When, however, he was confronted with the photograph his recognition was immediate. The lady, he announced, was Mrs. Fortesque who had occupied a room for a fortnight in the Spring of the previous year.

'And Mr. Fortesque?' Manson inquired.

'He was with Mrs. Fortesque, of course. He, in fact selected the Louvre and chose the room.'

'Some time in advance, undoubtedly?'

'No.' The manager flicked an imaginary speck of dust from a sleeve. 'They were staying at a hotel in Brighton the . . . er . . . amenities of which were not to their liking, and they were pleased to see that here the services were more to their liking.'

'I have no doubt they found it so,' Manson said, looking approvingly round the lounge. 'Do you know the name of the other establishment?'

'The Hotel Suisse is its description I believe.'

At the Suisse the staff knew nothing of a Mrs. Fortesque. Production of the photograph, however, brought quick recognition of the lady as Miss Whiting, who had stayed with them a week and then left paying a week's terms in lieu of notice. 'I thought she was Mrs. Fortesque,' explained

Doctor Manson at this surprise development.

The manageress smiled reminiscently.
'The mistake is a natural one, sir,' she
explained. 'Miss Whiting formed a warm
friendship for Mr. Fortesque who was
also a guest during her stay here. I have
often wondered' — she turned sentimen-
tal — 'whether they formed a permanent
attachment from this establishment.'

'Did you know Mr. Fortesque before
this particular visit?'

'Oh yes, indeed. He has stayed here on
many occasions, the last time at Christmas, when he was the life and soul of the
party.'

'What kind of man was he in
appearance?'

The manageress rummaged in a drawer
and produced a photograph of guests in
Christmas carnival attire. 'That,' she said,
pointing to a good-looking face topped
with a paper crown — 'is Mr. Fortesque.'

Under promise that it would be
returned, Doctor Manson slipped the
photograph into his case. Comparison of
it with the photograph of Mr. Brandon on

the visa application form at the U.S.A. Embassy showed no resemblance between the two. But when the aid of Superintendent Jones was sought, he identified the festive face as that which was still being worn by 'Black' Timmins. His demand to renew acquaintance with the owner was curbed by the Doctor.

'Bide a while, Fat Man,' he said. 'There is nothing against him so far except that he has registered at a hotel in a name other than his own. But that means only a fine, and nothing on which we could hold him.'

A telephone call to Mr. Swinburne led, however, to more concrete information. The Cissing lawyer stated that the £5,000 handed over to Miss Whiting had been paid into the South Provinces Bank in Oxford Street. A visit to the manager there disclosed the information that two cheques, each for £250, had been drawn by her in favour of a Mr. A. Timmins. One or two smaller sums had been drawn by Miss Whiting personally, and the remainder had been transferred with permission to the New York State

Bank in that city.

'Better talk to 'Black' now, Doctor,' suggested Jones.

'Yes, maybe we had, Fat Man,' the Doctor replied.

'Black' Timmins whose parents had, with obviously great expectations, christened him Alexander, lived on his wits. They were pretty good wits, too, for he lived at a rate corresponding to quite a few thousands a year. In his youth he had gone to a famous school, and then on to Oxford where he read Physics, but not for the full tale of years necessary for him to graduate; a drunken orgy in a low-class billiards hall landed him, first into the hands of the Bulldogs and then into the hands of the Dean of his college. Next day he was 'sent down', which is a euphemistical way of saying he was expelled from the university. It was this episode that started him on a life of crime.

With no more than a pound or two in his pocket, he went to London and booked a room in a famous hotel. A man of whom it could with justice be said that he was handsome, he had imbibed from his school and university that air of breeding, that atmosphere of *savoir faire*, and the easy and cultivated speech which is the heritage of the public school boy, however much that institution may be ridiculed and reviled. At the hotel he had posed as a partner in a City firm, talked of 'good things,' and quoted shares the names of which he had culled from a financial paper left on a seat in the train. And he found, to his amazement, that guests in the hotel, greedily ambitious to be behind the scenes, and impressed by his assurances, forced money upon him for the purchase on their behalf of the 'good things.' The total gifts paid his hotel bill and left him a three-figure sum for finance.

It was not long before Timmins realised that there was better and easier money to be got from women than from men. If they were women with money, they fell heavily so far as their wordly goods were concerned. An apparently wealthy young man and a 'Man about Town', attracted by their charm; flattered them, the more so if they were past the bloom of youth. One incident taught him that there was still more money to be made by compromising women and levying silence money. That was how he came by his designation 'Black' which is criminal and Scotland Yard language for blackmail, because twice he made mistakes. The first time he was sent to prison for three months; the next time to Pentonville for three years.

All this was, of course, known to Superintendent Jones and Inspector Kenway when Kenway led Timmins to the super's room in the Yard. The Inspector, paying a round of business calls, had come across him in the 'Game Cock' night club with a lady of decided charms and amorous intentions. The Amour vanished when Kenway introduced himself as an inspector of the C.I.D. So, too, did the lady.

In the Yard: 'Why did Aelthea Whiting pay you two sums, each of £250?' asked Superintendent Jones. '£500 in all,' he added as a mathematical afterthought.

'Come again,' Timmins said.

Jones jerked a finger at Kenway. 'You

tell him, inspector,' he said. 'He's so la-di-la he don't unnerstand me common language.' Kenway repeated the question.

'Aelthea Whiting?' Timmins screwed his brows into visible contortions of thought. 'Don't ever recall hearing the name, Super.'

Jones shook his head, sadly. 'All . . . 'like . . . clever fellers . . . thinks . . . dicks . . . halfwitted,' he said. His eyes stared aimlessly at the window, and through it to people walking along the Embankment. Crooks who saw and heard this phenomenon usually scratched bewildered heads thinking the fat police officer was talking to himself. 'That's it . . . he's . . . like 'em all,' the super meandered on. 'He'll . . . put . . . rope round his neck.' The superintendent's fingers ran round the rim of his collar, loosening it. Timmins swallowed hard, and Kenway seeing the man's Adam's Apple move up and down, grinned to himself.

'You never heard of the lady, eh?' Jones had come to himself with a loud voice. He fumbled in his desk and produced a memorandum. 'On May 10 last year, you stayed at the Louvre Hotel, Rottingdean, under the name of Fortesque. There was a Mrs. Fortesque. A week before that you were at the Suisse Hotel, Brighton, where a Miss Aelthea Whiting was staying. Mrs. Fortesque of the Louvre has been identified as Miss Whiting of the Suisse. On subsequent dates a maid employed in the home of Miss Whiting posted letters to a Mr. Fortesque at the Louvre Hotel, and afterwards to a London flat.'

The superintendent looked at his man and dived again into the desk. 'On 3rd June and June 19th respectively' — he pronounced each syllable of the word respectively — 'cheques were drawn by Miss Whiting in favour of a man named Timmins, and the endorsement is in your handwriting.' Once more his hand strayed to the drawer and came out with a photograph. 'This crowned king of the carnival' — the heavy humour rolled off his tongue — 'is the Mr. Fortesque of the Hotel Suisse — and is also 'Black' Timmins of the Hotel Pentonville.' He produced a page of writing and pointed to fingerprints standing out blackly.

'Some are those of Miss Whiting. But some of 'em are yours. Read the writing.' He pushed the page across the desk.

Timmins selected a cigarette and extended his gold case to the superintendent. And he was staggered when Fat Man took one and placed it on the desk. 'I'll smoke it when the air is a bit purer,' Jones announced. The stricken Timmins blew a smoke ring towards the ceiling. 'Haven't you forgotten to warn me, Super, that anything I say may be used in evidence? Or do you ignore Judge's Rules?'

'I'm not warning you — yet.'

'So I'm not being detained. The lady has gone to America. She has married. I hope she will be happy. Sure, she gave me a couple of cheques. A little present to ensure that our affair at the hotel should never be mentioned. A *present*, I said. She was very fond of me.'

'Took you a long time to recall her name, didn't it?'

'Not at all, old man. I said the cheques were a present so that our *affaire d'amour* should never be mentioned by me. I am a gentleman of honour. I volunteered nothing. You, my dear superintendent, have spilt the beans. Your evidence was too strong for me to deny.'

He picked up his hat and cane — and with a friendly wave walked out.

Doctor Manson heard the tale and commiserated with the police victim. 'Don't worry, Fat Man,' he said. 'You couldn't do any more. But keep him under your eye. He isn't clear of the wood yet. If things go well tonight, we'll have to get the lady back from America, and then we can put the two in front of each other.'

13

Four men entered the vault of the
Burstall family in the churchyard at
Cissing. It was midnight. In the dim light
of a hurricane lamp the mortal remains of
Eadwin Burstall were rudely disturbed
from their resting place. Mr. Abigail and
the scientist robed, masked and gloved
like disembodied spirits removed various
parts of his interior and placed them in
jars. The jars were sealed and labelled,
and signed by both men.

For the greater part of next day the
pathologist and Doctor Manson stood
over benches in the laboratory of a
Brighton hospital. Around them were a
littered array of glass tubes, jars, beakers,
Bunsen burners and bottles. Masked and
gloved again, they fingered the contents
of the jars that had been carried out of
the tomb of Burstall.

Looking . . . searching . . . for the
evidence they wanted. With all the

186

resources of modern toxicology, the knowledge of forensic medicine and forensic chemistry at their disposal, they sought for the secret of the death of the man whom they had so rudely disturbed.

One by one they applied the tests . . . sulphuric acid was added to test tubes containing fragments of viscera, and the men looked for any change of colour in the contents. Hydrochloric acid followed, and the Stras test followed that, and Grandean's test. And so it went on.

The two men worked slowly but patiently: for science and analysis cannot be hurried. Then at 4 p.m. the end came. They removed the masks and gloves, and returned by car to 'Hengeclif.'

Doctor Manson called Scotland Yard and waited a few moments for the A.C. to be fetched to the instrument. He spoke a few words in reply to the A.C.'s greeting.

'What!' The Voice of Sir Edward boomed out.

'What!' he said again. Then: 'Good Lord. Better come up and see me, Harry.'

'After we've had a meal, Edward,' the

Doctor promised. He wandered thought-fully back to the library where Mr. Abigail was waiting. He had reason to be thoughtful,

For . . .

No trace of poison had been found in the remains of Eadwin Burstall.

'We are now in a decided pickle,' the A.C. said. 'We practically had a murderer in our grasp — and now there is no murder.'

'I do not think we have grounds for that belief,' retorted Doctor Manson.

The news that no poison had been found in Burstall's body had come as a shock to Sir Edward. He felt he was likely to become the target for some hard speaking from the Home Secretary, after insisting on an exhumation. He turned again to Mr. Abigail. 'Could you have another go, if you think it worth while?' he asked.

'No, A.C.' said 'Stiffy'; and Doctor Manson nodded agreement.

'I mean to say,' the A.C. persisted, 'could there have been a secret poison that leaves no trace? I've heard of such a thing.'

'If . . . thunderin' . . . poison leaves . . . no trace . . . they couldn't find it.' Superintendent Jones, who had ruminated over this piece of basic knowledge, gave vent to the unspoken words of the expert and of Doctor Manson who had not liked to point out the obvious truth.

'All right,' Sir Edward admitted. 'WE were wrong, Doctor. And that's that. What do we do now?'

'We still have the forgery of the will.' The scientist made the remark quietly. 'But for the moment we will forget that. I am not yet admitting that we were wrong in believing that Eadwin Burstall was removed.'

'But, Doctor . . . ' Sir Edward began to interrupt. The Doctor waved to silence.

'Let me finish what I have to say A.C. The fact that no poison was found in the body does not exculpate both our suspects. If you remember I said some time ago that we had an *embarrass de richesse* in this case. It was necessary that we had to eliminate one of them.' He paused to let the fact sink into their minds. 'I have always held that the only way of solving crime is to eliminate, one by one, all the people who could *not* have committed it. The one who cannot be eliminated is the guilty person.'

'It has always worked very well,' the A.C. admitted.

'And there is no reason why it should not, eventually, work in this one. There was a quandary from the time we came across the list of poisons. The symptoms of the old man's last illness made it conceivable that one of the poisons had been used. Therefore, we had to ascertain whether he had, or had not, died of poison. Well, now we know that he did not die from the administration of *either of the poisons in the list* . . . '

'If you mean, Doctor, that we now have a negative result which is also a positive one . . . ' began Sir Edward.

'That is what I *do* mean.'

'Then Rawson is the man we want?'

'Not necessarily. But he must be eliminated.'

The A.C. wiped a moistened forehead. 'But he is the only one left.'

'So far as we know at present,' put in

Inspector Kenway, who by now had learned something of the working of the Doctor's mind.

'Quite right, Kenway. We'll make a logical detective of you yet. I personally think Rawson is the man we want, but I don't state it as a fact until I know it to *be* a fact. He may, for instance have had a confederate of whom as yet we know nothing. But he is, undoubtedly, the First Gravedigger.'

'Because he forged the will?' asked Mr. Abigail.

'Not because he forged it so much as the way he forged it,' replied the Doctor, cryptically.

The A.C. was studying the dossier of Rawson's part in the inquiry. 'In the statement of Mr. Swinburne,' the Doctor suggested, eyeing his chief. Sir Edward read through the precis. 'I see nothing bearing on it,' he protested.

Doctor Manson placed his fingers together in a tent and gazed at the ceiling. 'If I remember correctly, Mr. Swinburne said that after he had read the second will, Rawson now the beneficiary, asked him when the will was executed. The reply Swinburne made was, 'Apparently on January the tenth'.'

'That is so.' The A.C. marked the place with a thumb.

'That seemed to me remarkable,' Doctor Manson said. 'It first aroused my suspicions against Rawson.' He eyed each member of the company in turn, quizzingly. 'No?' he queried. 'Then let us get at it in another way. It may be reasonably assumed, I think, that if the will had been altered by Burstall himself in favour of his hereto disinherited nephew, it would be only on the basis that the nephew had come back into favour.'

'Agreed,' said Sir Edward.

'Now, according to Swinburne's and Forrestal's account of the incident — they were both quoting Miss Whiting — only one letter from Rawson ever arrived for her uncle after the break. Following that letter, and almost before they knew where they were, Rawson came to stay at the house. And uncle had not at any time written to Rawson until that one letter. In fact, there is no evidence except Rawson's that he ever did write that letter. But the fact remains, and this is important, that Rawson came to the house . . . '

'And ingratiated himself into uncle's favour,' the A.C. said.

'Continue, Sir Edward,' Manson encouraged. 'You're getting warm, as we used to say in Hunt the Slipper.'

The A.C. looked up, puzzled. 'Finished?' Manson asked. He looked round. 'All of you?'

There was no reply except from Jones who whispered to Kenway. 'Now look for the ruddy rabbit.'

'Doctor hasn't got a hat,' Kenway whispered back.

Doctor Manson heard the whispered dialogue, and looked round with a smile. 'The hat was always in front of you, and so was the rabbit. *Has it not occurred to you all that the date on which the new will was signed in favour of Rawson was a date anterior to that first visit of Astley to his uncle? In fact before he had ingratiated himself. Is that not in black and white in Swinburne's story of the scene in the library?*'

'That's ... one ... mistake ... all make,' boomed out Superintendent Jones.

'What is a mistake, Jones?' Doctor Manson asked. 'If the will was never discovered to be a forgery — and it is pure chance that it was so discovered — it is a strong point in his favour, for it suggests that for uncle to do such a thing before Rawson was back in favour, *he must have had grounds for disinheriting his niece.*'

'You mean had the will been changed after Rawson had come back there might have been a suggestion of undue influence?'

'Quite so. Rawson was in the position that he had to pre-date the will. So long as there was no suspicion of forgery the dating was safe. But the moment the forgery was established he was in a nasty hole. I see it this way: He could not have the will dated after he returned to the house. On the other hand, he could not leave the will with the prior date, or with any date, to be found in the desk by old Burstall, who would have gone up in the air and denounced his nephew. That is why I had to be sure that the old man was not poisoned. I was never convinced that he was so killed. Mind you, A.C., I have by no means cleared Aelthea Whiting of *intention to murder*. These poison notes meant something, and we know that she prepared them. I still believe that she thought Rawson was coming back into favour and if so, she would lose a great deal of the money that she hoped would have come to her. And she was under blackmail of some kind. I think that the death of Burstall forestalled her own attempt. And I don't think she has the least suspicion that his death meant that someone had got in front of her own decision to kill her uncle.'

The A.C. summed up: 'Rawson is the potential murderer because he forged the will — *ergo*, he was the one who had to put Burstall out of the way before the old man could make another will. Right, Doctor?'

'It is a logical hypothesis and one of which, of course, we shall have to work. But there are other avenues which will call for exploration.'

'How about Forrestal?' asked Superintendent Jones. 'He got £2,000.'

'Forrestal is pretty warm in money. There is, of course, an altruistic line. He was very fond of Aelthea Whiting and was at some concern over her dutiful attendance on the old man. He knew she wanted to get away, and may have thought that the tragedy of his own life, Burstall's daughter, was being repeated. And he saw the nephew back in favour.'

'We have to remember, Doctor,' Kenway put in, 'that he was hunting in the library.'

'And if there's anything that can be administered that doesn't leave traces, he being a doctor would know of it,' Jones chipped in.

'The one person who might be of use to us is Miss Whiting. She is far enough away to be unable to pass on any of our conversations with her — and too far away for us to get hold of,' Doctor Manson said.

'It would solve some of your difficulties if she could be spoken with, Doctor?' The query came from the A.C.

'I think it could be of real help.'

'You know her address in New York?'

'She would have to give her address where she was staying in New York.' He explained the U.S.A. Embassy visa requirements.

14

Doctor Manson stepped off a plane in New York at 10 o'clock in the morning. If you have never been to La Guardia airport you have missed an amazing experience of the modern world. For La Guardia is probably the best-equipped airport existing, and on its great stretch of tarmac and grass, planes land and take-off every ten minutes throughout the twenty-four hours of the day and night. There are giant airliners from the four quarters of the world; there are inter-state lines; there are private party planes, and there are flivvers of the air, which arrive and take-off as nonchalantly as in Britain a taxi-cab is hailed, or a car parked in a side street.

Take a typical arrival about 5.30 p.m. on a summer afternoon. A little plane, painted blue and white, tips down on the near centre runway. Its door opens and a man and woman in evening dress step out. The man with the air of a port mechanic, wheels the little machine into a parking line a few yards away, and off the couple go to a theatre. Four or so hours later they return, push their flivver back onto the tarmac, step in, start up the motor and a few minutes later will be winging their way back home — 200 or 300 miles away. You will see that at La Guardia twenty times in an evening.

From the airport Doctor Manson passed through the Customs, to the car park with its customary thousand cars in rows that give instant access to the highway. He hired a taxi-cab. 'Jackson Heights . . . 37th Avenue,' he directed.

Thirty-seventh avenue is a wide, tree-lined street with shops. Over much of its length the New York Elevated Railway runs its clanging, intolerably noisy course. It is a relic of Old New York when there were a dozen of these sun and sky-hiding monstrosities — now there remain but two.

Mrs. Brandon, Aelthea Whiting had given an address in the avenue; and there Doctor Manson found her. She looked out from the door of an apartment on the second floor of a block on his ring. For a moment she stared at him in inquiry, and then recognition came.

'Good gracious, it is Mr. Manson,' she said. 'What a surprise, and how did you find me. Come inside.' She led him into the lounge of her apartment and pulled up an armchair. 'I thought you were still recuperating in Cissing,' she said.

'I am, in theory, Mrs. Brandon.' The Doctor smiled slightly. 'I should be there now, except that I had to fly to see you on a matter of some urgency.'

'Urgency . . . me?' The woman frowned in bewilderment. 'Whatever can you want to see me about?'

It was then that the Doctor played his opening gambit. He had devoted the hours of his journey from London debating in what way he should begin an interview with a woman in whom he knew had been born the desire to rid herself of an incumbrance. After careful cogitation he decided that a shock such as he knew that his knowledge of her mind would give, would probably best suit his purpose. He now struck the blow:

'Tell me, Mrs. Brandon, when did you finally give up your idea of poisoning Mr. Eadwin Burstall?'

She slumped back in her chair as though she had been shot. For the space of a minute she presented the appearance of catalepsy. Slowly, very slowly she recovered. She sat up, her eyes burning in intensity; and she spoke.

Manson listened to her tirade in silence only of tongue; his brain was busy noting the colour slowly fading from the woman — first from her face and then creeping down her neck in pallor until she showed nearly grey under her cosmetics. In her neck the great vein was throbbing. These are the tell tale signs which no woman can hide, however great an actress over her passions she may be. When sheer exhaustion intervened to silence her, Doctor Manson spoke again.

'I know too much to worry over denials, Mrs. Brandon,' he said. 'And I have these' — the pages of the notebook appeared in his hands — 'with your fingerprints on.' He pointed them out, gently. 'And here are two prints of Mr. Timmins. These are what you were searching for when I came to the house. You see, I had seen you from outside the library window before I entered the house by the front door. And they are what Esther and Doctor Forrestal tried to find, are they not?'

She nodded, dumbly.

'I also know of the Brighton and Rottingdean hotels incidents, and the cheques given to Timmins, who was Fortesque.'

'I see.' The words came lifelessly from her, and she slumped again in her chair. Her eyes wandered listlessly and lustreless round the pretty room. 'I see,' she said again, bitterly. 'And now you come to see me. I have nothing left,' she went on. 'Nearly all that I had left of my legacy went in paying the other man and furnishing this — my home. My husband knows nothing of my past.' Her voice was toneless and as dead as the grave.

Doctor Manson was shocked to his feet. 'Good heavens, Mrs. Brandon, do you suppose I came here to blackmail you,' he said.

'What else have you come for. What interest can it be to anyone except as a means of revenue?'

'But — ' the scientist looked the surprise he felt. 'Do I understand you are not aware of my identity?'

'I know, of course, that you are Mr. Manson.'

'Doctor Manson is the correct description, Mrs. Brandon, and I am attached as scientific adviser to Scotland Yard. Now, don't let that worry you,' he added hastily. Mention of Scotland Yard had sent a hand to her mouth, and terror welled into her eyes. 'There is nothing you need fear from me. Suppose you answer the question I first asked and then we can talk. When did you finally give up your idea of poisoning Mr. Burstall?'

Mrs. Brandon hesitated. The dread had not altogether departed from her mind, though it had been soothed by the scientist's attitude. She had wit enough to realise that she had not, so far, made any admission of guilty intent; but an answer to the question in the form in which it had been put would be such an admission, since she could not give up that which she never had any intention of committing. In a minute, the space of which seemed like an eternity, she made her decision.

'*When my uncle died*, Doctor Manson.' The answer came softly. 'But I do not think I should ever have carried it out. My courage would have failed me.'

A thought crossed her mind. After all, her visitor was from Scotland Yard and had flown from London to see her. 'You don't think I *did* poison uncle, do you?'

'I know you did not,' was the reply. 'There was no poison in the body.'

'In his body?' Mrs. Brandon stared. 'Do you mean — '

'Exhumed him? Yes, we had to, you know, having found what we did.' He indicated the list of poisons. 'You know, of course, that either of these, administered, would have simulated the illness from which your uncle was suffering?'

'Yes, I had studied them for that.'

'Now, Mrs. Brandon, you realise of

course that we know pretty well your story. Our reading of it is that you were being blackmailed by Timmins and were driven to the lengths of thinking of poisoning Mr. Burstall in order to get your inheritance under the will and thus be able to pay the blackmailer. Your uncle surprised you by dying . . .'

'It was a dreadful surprise, Doctor Manson. Doctor Forrestal had said that there was no likelihood of him dying only two days before.'

'Now, this list of poisons. I have been speculating how you came to leave them in a book in the library. I think, probably, the explanation is that you had been studying the poisons with the aid of the encyclopaedia in the library, and on some occasion had been surprised by an unexpected entrance into the room . . .'

'My uncle,' she said.

' . . . And you slipped your notes into a book of which you were too hurried to note the title. Afterwards you searched for the book and could not find it. Did you confide the nature of the pages to Doctor Forrestal?'

She nodded. 'I had to tell him what I had intended to do. He told Esther they were some papers he had lent me and I had lost them. That is how she came to be searching for them. Did he tell you about them?'

'Who? Doctor Forrestal? No, I assure you he kept the secret. He does not know that I know about them. Now, all this is very much as I had worked it out, Mrs. Brandon. What I do not understand is how Timmins or, as you first knew him, Fortesque, came to know all about the planned poisoning.'

The story now told by Mrs. Brandon was easily recognisable by the police scientist as the customary *modus operandi* of a man who lives on the dividends of blackmail. She had been a couple of days at the Hotel Suisse when Fortesque struck up an acquaintance with her. He was a presentable man, good company, who seemed to be a welcome guest at the hotel.

'He knew who I was,' she said, 'and he also knew Cissing; he mentioned a number of people in the place who were known to me as of good standing.' She said they became secretly engaged. Fortesque explained that he was the director and principal shareholder in a firm of electrical engineers, but did not take much part in the active working of the business, having a sufficient income to enjoy himself.'

'And, of course, he suggested that you and he went to the Louvre Hotel as man and wife? It is the old trick of a man who is proposing to blackmail a woman who he has reason to think has money, or is likely to have money, and would not face scandal in a small place where she and her family are known. When did he first begin to demand money?'

She said it was some months later. He had borrowed sums from her when he had forgotten his cheque book. As he made no offer to repay, she began to have doubts of his character. Then she met Mr. Brandon and found her feelings for him were higher than for Fortesque. She told Fortesque she no longer cared for his company.

'He suggested we should meet in

Brighton for a good-bye talk,' she said, 'and then he asked me whether I thought he should tell his friend Brandon about the Rottingdean incident.'

'He did not know Brandon, of course?'

Mrs. Brandon shook her head. 'Then he said his business was doing badly, and he wanted money. That was the start of my paying him.' She said she gave him practically all her allowance. He demanded more and said she would have thousands of pounds when her uncle died, which wouldn't be very long now, and he agreed to wait until that event if she would sign an IOU for £500.

'I was in despair,' she said. 'Uncle was taken ill . . . '

'And in desperation you thought of the idea of using the illness to hasten his death. When did Timmins, as I suppose you now knew him, come to see the poison list?'

'He came to Cissing and telephoned me to meet him in the churchyard. I said I had no money left. He snatched my handbag and looked through it. The notes were in the bag. He looked at them and said I was obviously going to do away with uncle to get the money, as I was the heiress. He knew that, he said, because he knew someone in Mr. Swinburne's office.'

'I see. Tell me, Mrs. Brandon, did you know of the existence, or suspect the existence of the new will?'

'I had not the least suspicion. I have been glad ever since that uncle died. I might have committed murder for nothing. That's why I was not really upset when the money went to William. I thought it was a judgement on me for my thoughts and plotting.' She sat back, her story finished; but a thought struck her, and she leaned forward again. 'But you seem to have known this, sir. And you said there was no poison in uncle's body. You say you know I did not kill him. Then why have you come all this way to see me?'

'*Because, Mrs. Brandon, we think that somebody else did bring about his death, and we think you may be able to help us in our investigations, and find out who.*'

'He *was* killed . . . Oh.' She burst into

tears. 'Do you mean that Timmins killed him in order that I should come into the money?'

'If he did he must be a very disappointed man. Tell me, did Timmins ever come to see you in Cissing and did he have access to the house?'

'Oh, no. We met once or twice at night, but I would never have dared admit him to the house.'

'He could not have taken your key when he snatched your handbag that day?'

She shook her head. 'I did not carry the key in my bag. But how could he kill uncle when there was no sign on uncle?'

'There are ways in which a man's heart can be so disturbed that death will ensue. What I am trying to account for is the sudden collapse of Mr. Burstall after Doctor Forrestal had stated there was no likelihood of his dying. Can you give me some idea of the habits of your uncle during those last few weeks? How did he, for instance, spend his time?'

'Mostly in the garden until he became

too much out of breath, then in the library. Mostly William was with him and they spent all the evening talking over business and drinking. I often wonder whether all the whisky he drank did him any harm.'

'Did he take soda with it?'

'No, only water. Vasey medicinal water it was. William had whisky and ginger ale. He said one could drink more whisky with ginger ale.'

'I believe you can — for a time. What did Esther think of these goings-on?'

'Esther did not see much of it. She went to bed early after she had caried the bottles into the library.'

'Bottles?' Doctor Manson looked incredulous.

'What, whisky? Did they get through that much in a night?'

'Oh no. Not bottles of whisky. It was bottles of water, and the ginger ale.'

'I see. But why bottles of water?'

'Uncle had medicinal water. Like Vichy, you know, only this was Vasey water or some name like that.'

'I take it you knew nothing about the

business between your uncle and your cousin?'

'No. It was never mentioned by them. Doesn't Mr. Swinburne know?'

'No. There was no record of any business in the papers that were left.' The Doctor rose to his feet. 'Then I think that is all you can tell me,' he said. He held out a hand. 'Good-bye, and I hope you will be happy in your new life. Forget all you have told me today — I shall forget it myself. There is no reason why you should ever hear of it again. If by any chance you should hear from Timmins, will you promise to let me know at once, and I will soon put an end to his tricks.'

On the air journey back to London, the Doctor ruminated over the whim of fate which would soon turn again towards the woman who thought the past could ever die; it would be resurrected in the not distant future when the will of Eadwin Burstall was pronounced a forgery, and the earlier will put into her hands the fortune which once she had thought to obtain by poison, and in which that same fate had intervened — kindly.

Sir Edward Allen and Doctor Manson travelled down to Cissing on a typical English summer's afternoon — which means to say it was raining and the sky was pigeon-grey with a chilling wind. The A.C. on the way down heard the result of the trip to New York. 'Would she have poisoned the man, do you think?' he asked.

'Hard to say, Edward. She might have been driven by force of circumstances to carry out her intentions. Poison is a woman's weapon; has been since the days of Lucretia Borgia. But let's forget her. She's no good to us.'

'And Timmins? Is he any good to us?'

'That remains to be seen. I have been worrying about him since I heard Mrs. Brandon's story. He is, I feel, on the chequer-board, but in what position I cannot place. Look at the facts: How much money had Miss Whiting? A few pounds allowance. Does Timmins, as we know him, spend a considerable sum on hotels and so on to blackmail a woman for her allowance? We know him better than that.'

Sir Edward snorted. 'He knew she was an heiress.'

Doctor Manson nodded. 'I had not overlooked the point, Edward, nor have I failed to remind myself that the heiress was of no use to Timmins until Burstall was dead. And shortly afterwards, Burstall *was* dead. Furthermore, Timmins was in the area, actually within a few yards of the house, shortly before Burstall *did* die.'

'But he didn't kill him.' The retort came from the A.C. 'There is no way of killing a man without leaving a trace of murder of some kind. Timmins could only strangle, poison or knock him over the head with a sharp or blunt instrument. Burstall had no fracture of the skull, he was not cut, and he wasn't poisoned.'

'Wrong, A.C.' Merry said. 'There's another way.'

'Yes. Scare him to death, I suppose!'

'No. But he could kill him by an air-lock. All that is wanted is an empty syringe.' The Doctor nodded in harmony. 'It could be done, and it *has* been done. Only Burstall wasn't,' he added.

'That definite?' the A.C. asked.

'Certain. Embolism brings out a sudden collapse of the victim. Burstall died quietly according to all we hear. He went down quickly, it is true, but he did not die a sudden death.'

'Well, then, that seems to clear Timmins. Let's turn to Rawson.'

Merry, who had spent the preceding forty-eight hours importuning into the back life and habits of William Rawson put the tale of his discoveries into words.

★   ★   ★

William Rawson was the son of the elder of the two sisters of Eadwin Burstall, and Aelthea Whiting was the daughter of the younger. Both mothers had found one child a sufficient family: or perhaps the discovery belonged to their husbands. Whichever claimed the credit the fact remained that the nephew and niece of old Eadwin were 'only children.' Now, whereas the men of the Burstall family had invariably reaped a profitable harvest from life, the Burstall women seemed fated to take less from existence than they put into it. Both the sisters of old Eadwin married men who came to no estate either of land or money; whereas Eadwin Burstall had added considerably to the money bequeathed to him by his father as his share. The misfortune of the women still lingered even to Aelthea Whiting; she had come to the charity of 'Hengeclif', even as William Rawson had come, some time earlier.

Rawson had been sent to a well-known public school, but Uncle Eadwin was having no truck with the expense of a university. Accordingly, at the end of his last school term Rawson had entered 'Hengeclif'. It was not at all likely that he would be allowed to remain there indefinitely, but whatever views Eadwin Burstall had for his future were forestalled by seeing the back of him. He was turned out of the house with sufficient money to support him until he could find a job which would ensure him a livelihood. None but Rawson himself and Burstall, and possibly Mr. Swinburne, knew the offence which closed the

'Hengeclif' doors to him; Swinburne had on one occasion mentioned in a moment of forgetfulness something about a cheque, but suddenly realising what he had said clamped down before he had revealed enough to qualify for an explanation . . .

'So he came to London,' said the A.C. He said it with considerable feeling. 'He *would*. Every Tom, Dick and Harry crook comes to London, and I have to run round catching them.'

'Must have nearly worn out your poor feet, Edward,' said Doctor Manson. Merry chuckled at the spectacle of the elegantly groomed Sir Edward chasing after wrong-doers all over the Metropolis.

'How much did he get away with, and what happened to him in London, Jim?' asked Manson.

'How much uncle compounded his inheritance for I don't know, but it must have been a tidy sum, because Rawson seems to have taken a bachelor flat in Jermyn Street, and immediately began to do himself well in the way of wine, women and song . . . '

'Say wine and women,' suggested the A.C. 'No man ever did himself well with song. Rawson's patrimony wouldn't go far in those circumstances. Where did he get money?'

'Playing the bookies, I'm told. I should say he had been betting at school and at uncle's, because he appears to have known the ropes. The Jermyn Street address was a good one . . . '

'Inspired confidence, of course,' the A.C. commented. 'It was a street of weathy young men, wasn't it, Harry?'

'In those days, yes,' agreed Manson.

Merry proceeded: 'He seems to have opened accounts with a number of bookmakers, unknown to one another, of course. At first he won a bit and lost a bit, and always paid up his losses on settling day. That and his elegant appearance got him a good maximum for last minute telephoned bids at starting price, if you get me. Then he plunged with each one on a coup, took his winnings and didn't pay his losses. I am told he got away with more than £7,000 . . . Did you speak, Sir Edward?'

'I didn't, but I will do so. I seem to remember the happening. Was he the young man sued for debt by one of the bookmakers?'

'Right, Sir Edward. He pleaded the Gaming Act, but the bookie . . .'

'Of course! I've got it. The bookmaker claimed that the case had been lifted out of the Gaming Act by a letter from Rawson promising to pay when he could. Rawson lost the case, judgement being given for the bookmaker, and then the young scoundrel sprang the bombshell that he was a minor and could not be sued in any case. That correct?'

'Quite correct, Sir Edward.'

'So he had something over £7,000, but he was, of course, finished in that line of business. How long ago was this, Jim?' Doctor Manson asked.

'About five years ago, Doctor. That just about finishes my part of the story. Superintendent Jones was on the later career of Rawson.'

Sir Edward cleared his throat. 'That is so, Doctor. Now Jones says . . .' He produced a typewritten report from a pocket and skimmed through it to refresh his memory. 'Ah, yes, Jones says that Rawson became a car salesman for a West End firm. He was given a demonstration car for his own use which same, being driven by him pretty nearly everywhere in the West End, gave the general impression that he was a young man of very considerable means. And on that standing he secured credit in West End hotels for meals at which he did a lot of entertaining. He also obtained expensive luxuries on credit. The car selling ceased when the firm found out he was fiddling them on cheques as well as getting commisions on sales . . . '

'He seems to have been a genius at diddling hard-headed business men,' Manson said. 'Car dealers and bookmakers. He didn't by any chance go in for horse doping in his racing days, did he?'

'There's nothing about horses. But doping may be a good bet. He was suspected of something of the sort in connection with the Nighthawk Night Club. He drew commission for touting for the club among well-to-do foreign tourists who wanted a little game of excitement. Baccarat and Chemin were played in private back rooms. You may remember that it was said that most of the losses of those gentry were due to a judicious supply of dope in the drinks sold in the rooms.'

The A.C. consulted the dossier again. 'From then on, Jones says, he appeared to be living on air. He did nothing wrong that we know of, but didn't seem to be doing anything right, either. He supported what Old Fat describes as ' a bit of glamorous homework' . . . '

'Dodo Havering.' Merry chipped into the tale. 'I know all about her.' Catching Doctor Manson's quizzing gaze and insinuating cough, he added, hastily, 'from friends of mine, not personally.'

'When you've finished with your blondes, I'll continue,' the A.C. said, patiently. 'Then a few months ago Rawson vanished from his haunts. He came back on a date which ties up round about the death of Burstall, stayed a few weeks, and then vanished again to Monte Carlo, where he still is. That is all Jones knows,' Sir Edward concluded, and passed the dossier over to the Doctor.

'Do I gather that he still occupies the Jermyn Street flat?' Manson inquired.

'No, no, Doctor.' Merry hastened to complete the story. 'That went after the bookmaking *débâcle*. He lived in various places after that, but before he reappeared in Cissing he had a flat in the Edgware Road, near St. John's Wood, and he still has it. He shared it with another fellow.'

'Another?' Doctor Manson looked up sharply. 'Who?'

'No idea, except that his name is Greenwell, Peter Greenwell, according to the landlady — she lives in the basement and Rawson has the top flat — the couple had a row and Rawson turned Greenwell out of the place. He changed the locks on the door and told her that Greenwell was not to be allowed in the place again. Greenwell has appeared there several times, and last time had to be turfed off the premises by the landlady's husband.'

Doctor Manson digested the story. 'And what is the business in which Eadwin Burstall was interested and which

Rawson brought to this house and room in which we are sitting' — he indicated the library in which they were talking.

'Haven't the foggiest idea.' Merry spread his hands. 'Nor has Jones. The woman at the flat nearly dropped with shock when we asked her. It staggered her that anyone should think Mr. Rawson was ever engaged in any kind of business. Jones says questions on the topic were greeted with derision by all who knew Rawson.'

'And the man friend is no longer *en rapport?*'

'Has not been seen round for some time. He is apparently another non-worker.'

The A.C. snorted. 'Never did think much of the 'business' story anyway.'

'No?' Doctor Manson laughed. 'You surprise me, Edward. The business was, undoubtedly, the means of Rawson getting back, firstly to see his uncle, and then to remain here. And it had to be shown in some form sufficiently good to impress old Eadwin, who was no fool and didn't trust Rawson anyway. There had to be some suggestion of a business, or an undertaking and Rawson had to provide some detail and outline.'

'You mean he had to get into this place to plant the will?' said Merry.

'Why could he not send it to the lawyer?' The A.C. made the suggestion.

'Because Swinburne would have acknowledged receipt — to Burstall, Edward. And it would have been good-bye again to nephew William — especially as he had once before played uncle a trick with a cheque.'

'Now, we're back where we started.' Sir Edward viewed the position with metaphorical lachrymation. There is no sign that the old man died of anything but a natural death. You've even destroyed my loophole of a secret poison that leaves no trace.'

'Burstall *was* killed — of that I am certain. He had to be killed. Since at present a man cannot be killed by long distance telepathy or suggestion, access had to be gained to this house in order to obtain opportunity.'

'But how, Harry. *How*?'

'I think we ought to get into that flat,' the Doctor said to Kenway, later. 'There may be something there that will help. Whatever Rawson did must have been planned and executed in there — his home before he came down here to uncle.'

15

Rawson's flat lay in the Edgware Road, just short of St. John's Wood Road, which runs up to Lord's Cricket Ground. It was not in one of the numerous blocks of flats, but occupied the top floor of a residence, a relic of Edwardian days, when homes were built stoutly and solidly, with massive stone facings.

Doctor Manson and Chief Detective Inspector Kenway walked up the three ornamental stone steps and rang the bell. It was answered by a puffing and panting woman, the figure of whom could only faithfully be reproduced by tying a rope round the middle of a bulging sack and standing it upright.

'Mrs. Biggs?' inquired Doctor Manson.

The buxom woman answered the indictment. 'That's me.'

'Ah!' The Doctor conveyed an expression of complete and thankful satisfaction in his voice. He produced an envelope from a pocket and tapped it with a finger. 'Mr. Rawson's landlady, of course. We have called to see Mr. Rawson's flat with a view of renting it from him furnished. William, you know, is in the South of France. He is not thinking of coming back yet — and we want a resting-place while we are in London.'

'Well, sir, that's a bit of a surprise. He hasn't written to me about letting the place.'

'He hasn't had time. Only suggested it to us in this letter this morning. We would like to see the place, of course before we say yea or nay. It might not be comfy enough for us.'

A guffaw greeted this. 'You ain't no need to worry about that, sir. Mr. Rawson was allus one for his bit of comfort. Very posh his place is. But come inside, and I'll get me keys.'

Doctor Manson dug Kenway in the ribs. 'There you are, you see. Easy as pie.'

'Mebbe, Doctor, but what the A.C. would say if he knew is nobody's business. It's strictly against the rules.'

'With only a modicum of luck, my lad,

he need never know. And anyway, when it's done, it's done,' he added with a chuckle. 'Hush, here she is.'

The woman appeared at the head of the basement stairs, panting again. 'Stairs . . . be the death of me . . . bronchitis, you know, sirs.'

'And now you have to climb to the top of the house,' commiserated Manson. 'Rawson told me he had the top flat. Now look here. Don't you come all the way. I think you can trust us not to go off with the furniture. If you like to entrust us with the keys we'll look over the flat and come back here. You take care of our hats and coats in the meantime.'

She hesitated. 'Oh, I suppose it will be all right, sir, you knowing Mr. Rawson. As a matter of fact I'm glad you've called. I've written to him twice for some money. There's the gas and electricity owing, wot he didn't pay before he went away, and they keeps coming for the money.'

'I'm not surprised. How long has he been away? Some weeks isn't it? Well, if we take the flat we'll find the money and deduct it from the rent he charges us.

How much are the bills, by the way?'

'The gas bill is only just over two pounds, but the electricity is more than £30.'

'That seems an extraordinary large amount. Is it generally as large as that?'

'Only the last few times, sir.'

They took the keys and climbed to the top floor. Manson turned the key and threw open the door. He placed a restraining hand on Kenway's shoulders. 'Just a moment,' he said, 'let's have a clear look before we go inside.' He gazed into what was obviously the sitting-room of the flat.

'Did himself very well, didn't he?' said Kenway after a quick ocular examination of the set-up of the room. A thick-piled russet brown carpet covered the floor. Leather armchairs occupied cosy sites on each side of the fireplace, and a settee rested against the wall opposite. There was an oak sideboard and a cocktail cabinet. The Doctor, having filled his eyes with the *ensemble* opened the doors of the cocktail cabinet to reveal a collection of appetizer concoctions, complete with glasses and a shaker. A period desk stood crossways in a corner. It was locked. Smiling at his inspector's expression, the Doctor produced an instrument from one of his pockets, fiddled in the lock with it, and a moment later the flap was gently lowered on to its supports.

'Oh, crumbs!' said Kenway.

Rapidly the Doctor went through the contents of the pigeonholes. 'Letters . . . photos . . . would amuse Merry,' he said shovelling a collection of ladies in various states of undress back into a compartment. 'Nothing here of any use as far as I can see.'

'What's this, Doctor?' Kenway, who had joined in the scrutiny, had been examining three or four sheets of paper clipped together with a stapling machine. The sheets of paper were marked with foldings.

'Been carried round in pockets, and has been folded and unfolded by two people.' Doctor Manson said.

'Why different people?'

'Elementary observation.' He exhibited the sheets. 'You see how the folds vary.

The only possible explanation for that is that the original owner first folded the sheets in a certain way, sent or gave it to another person who similarly folded it, but did so by beginning at the opposite end of the papers. You will find that most people after reading through a paper before enclosing it in an envelope invariably fold it in a certain way — what I mean is that they turn in the bottom fold first, or top fold downwards. It becomes an unconscious idiosyncrasy. *And he seldom changes the order.* These sheets have been folded in three different ways.'

The two bent over and read through the entries on the four sheets. 'Curious,' Kenway said at the end. 'They look like some kind of accounts with no named items.'

Manson vouchsafed no reply. He scrutinised closely the items, and compared the entries on the second, third and fourth sheets, occasionally nodding his head in satisfaction. 'They are, indeed, curious, Kenway,' he said at last. 'As strange a collection of documents as I have seen. So far as I can judge the accounts show transactions over an unnamed period, and represent profit which it is suggested amounts to about 700 per cent. It is strange enough that any concern should show a profit to that extent; but it is even more strange that the items in the account should not be named, and that the name of the concern should not appear anywhere in the accounts.'

'Looks to me, Doctor, as if there is something underhand in the business.'

'Um! Might it not suggest that anyone accepting these figures as a genuine trade account has no check whatever on the authenticity of this document?' the Doctor suggested. 'If you possessed any considerable amount of money, and someone brought you a genuine under-taking from which you could receive a return of 700 per cent, what would be your reaction?'

'To bung some cash into it — quickly.'

'If the accounts shown you were such as those, would you invest then?'

'Not ruddy likely.'

'I wonder!' the Doctor said — and ruminated aloud. 'You are a business man, avaricious by nature. You are offered an investment of 700 per cent return, and when you complain that the figures here present no stamp of unimpeachability about them, what are you told? 'What do you suppose we are. Do you suppose we get 700 per cent from any above-board transactions? We are engaged in something shady, and we aren't writing our names, or anything else, on paper which could get into wrong hands and be used in evidence against us. These are our accounts and we have told you by word of mouth how they are obtained. You take them or leave them, we don't mind which. We're letting you into the game because you've got money, and with money we can do even better, and increase our profits. If you don't want to come in, that's all right with us, we'll find somebody who will.' What do you say to that, Kenway?'

'*That a man like Eadwin Burstall, from what I have heard of him, would fall for it, Doctor.*'

'And,' Manson said, 'it offers a reasonable explanation of why no memoranda of the business in which he was engaged with Rawson was among the possessions left behind on his death. Anyway, we'd better finish our search.'

They returned to the sitting-room and opened another of the doors. It led into the kitchen, an oblong-shaped room some twelve feet by ten. A sink was sited in front of and beneath the window, and on either side of the window shelves were fitted for plates and cups and saucers. There was a small gas cooker. A fireplace occupied a corner of the kitchen, the chimney stack jutting out into the room. It had the effect of leaving a recess stretching across the remainder of the width of the kitchen. Built into this recess was a large cupboard running from floor to ceiling. It was closed with a door. Manson pulled at the door, which remained closed.

'Locked,' he said. 'Probably his store cupboard and he is taking care Mrs. Biggs is not tempted to share its contents.' The same curious little instrument that had opened the desk appeared again in his fingers, and a moment later the door was opened. An exclamation of surprise came from the Doctor. Kenway moved across and looked over his shoulder.

'What the devil is it?' he said.

The interior of the cupboard was divided by stout wooden shelves into three compartments. In the bottom (floor) compartment the back consisted of a panel board holding gauges and meters. There were also test tubes, lengths of cable and flex, several switches and a number of bottles.

On the middle shelf was a large apparatus some four feet high and six feet long. It was apparently in two components, joined by a thick glass tube which spiralled into the second part of the apparatus. The spiral section, however, was enclosed in a much wider glass 'jacket' which narrowed at the entrance and exit. A rubber tubing ran from entrance and exit of the jacket and passed through a side of the cupboard. Doctor Manson, following it, located the two ends as hanging underneath the sink. A

15-amp power cable ran from the instrument down to a plug in the lower part of the cupboard. The sides and shelf of the compartment were lined with asbestos sheets.

Doctor Manson next turned his attention to the upper compartment. It contained another apparatus of an entirely different kind. A large container stood neglected in a corner. Near it lay electric arcs made of carbon. There was also more chemical apparatus, similar, to that in the bottom part. This shelf, too, was asbestos lined.

'It looks like a blessed engineering works in miniature, Doctor,' Kenway said. 'What the devil is it?'

Now, Manson's Doctorate of Science had been earned by his great knowledge of all branches of scientific investigation, not confined to criminal activities, and the years since he had taken it from Cambridge he had spent in research in laboratories and books. He passed the rule of his knowledge over the cupboard in the flat — and found himself defeated to a great extent by it.

'I have no clear idea what it is,

Kenway,' he confessed. 'I cannot for the life of me understand its purpose. The apparatus on the top shelf is for electrolysis. That is not unusual in itself, but the arrangement is somewhat different. Were the container filled with water and the apparatus used, the result would be to send an electric current through the water. When this operation is done water is split into hydrogen and oxygen. There seems to have existed some connection between that process and the contraption underneath. But until I know the reason for the electrolysis I am at a loss to account for its necessity.'

'And what is that one?' Kenway pointed to the middle shelf.

'That, Kenway, is easier. It is what is called a fractioniting still. It can be worked under reduced pressure, but there are other accessories which I don't understand. It looks to me an improvement of a remarkable nature, and certainly the work of a man who knows more than a little of some branch of physics.'

'Rawson, Doctor?'

'All I am prepared to say is that if it *is* Rawson, then we have gravely misjudged that young man . . . '

He was interrupted by an exclamation from his companion. 'Did you say that part is a still, Doctor?' he asked.

'I did. It is a still of some kind.'

'And Rawson is in some business, or supposed to be, paying 700 per cent dividend. What is a still for, Doctor?'

'Well, it is used for a number of varied operations including the one of which you have thought suddenly' — he smiled 'making illicit liquor.'

'Well, there you are, Doctor.'

'Only you see, Kenway, it is, firstly, not a big enough still to earn those dividends; and, secondly, there is no trace whatever of the raw materials for the distilling of moonshine; there is not even a speck or an ear or a grain of anything. You cannot distil it from the air, you know.'

They delivered up the keys, and set out for the Yard. As they walked along the Edgware Road in the direction of the tube station, the wrinkles gathered on the forehead of the Doctor, and crinkles came into the corners of his eyes. 'What I can't understand, Kenway,' he said, 'is that there is no evidence that anything is being made there except distilled water. Why should anyone set up all that paraphernalia to distil water when you can buy the stuff by the gallon at any garage service station?'

16

Though Doctor Manson possessed an equable disposition and temper, there was one circumstance which never failed to call from him a surge of caustic comment. That circumstance was an attempt on the part of his Yard colleagues to put forward some theory or other of a crime in order to set about searching for the offender against the law.

He had no objection to theorising — so long as the theorising was based solely on the facts put in front of him. But theorising of that kind, he had frequently pointed out, was a different kiddle of fish to theorising and then setting out to make the facts fit the theory. Accordingly, he made it as rigid a law as those of the Medes and the Persians to gather as many facts as he could before proceeding to analyse the case under investigation, and draw conclusions to help on the investigations.

On his return to Cissing, where Merry

who was still on guard, and from the Edgware Road flat, the Doctor decided that he now held all the facts concerning the death of Eadwin Burstall that it was possible for him to obtain. He had accumulated them one by one, gathering up loose ends here and there, as they became apparent.

Accordingly, with the assistance of Inspector Merry, he reviewed his knowledge in notative order. The two men set them down in tabulated form.

FACT 1: Eadwin Burstall died unexpectedly. Doctor Forrestal did not expect him to die, and had said so.
Theory on this: He must have been helped off.

FACT 2: A list of poisons was discovered for which three persons had searched. It belonged to Aelthea Whiting (Now Mrs. Brandon). Each of the poisons could have caused death with approximately the same symptoms diagnosed as present in the victim.

FACT 3: Mrs. Brandon had expected to inherit her uncle's estate.

Theory on this: The poisoning fitted facts 1–3. Tested, however, all proved unfounded; there was no poison found in Burstall.

'Which wipes out all the facts except Fact one,' said Merry.

'Agreed,' the Doctor said, and drew a second sheet of paper, and started again. He wrote:

FACT 1: Eadwin Burstall died, unexpectedly.

FACT 2: After his death a will was found under which William Rawson, the nephew, inherited the estate which Mrs. Brandon had expected would come to her.

FACT 3: The will is proved to be a forgery.

FACT 4: The will was found in Burstall's desk, where he could at any time have come across it with fatal results to Rawson.

Theory: It was certainly placed there after the old man's death. Since it benefitted only Rawson, it may be concluded he did the placing.

PERSONALITIES CONCERNED

MRS. BRANDON: Was being blackmailed by 'Black' Timmins, who understood her to be the heiress and had compromised her in a manner usual to him. He had seen the poison list in her possession.

She admitted to thinking of poisoning her uncle, being desperate for money, and thinking she was the heiress to the estate, but said she did not do so, because she had not the courage.

Comment: I believe her story.

'BLACK' TIMMINS: Was interested in the death of Burstall. Successful blackmail was only possible when Mrs. Brandon came into the estate. He had already had her allowance in blackmail, and is known to have been in the

neighbourhood of the house at the time of death, and may have gained access.

Comment: There is no evidence that he ever came into contact with Burstall, and there were no marks of violent death on Burstall.

WILLIAM RAWSON: Forged a will giving him the inheritance, and introduced it into the house to be found after death. Suspicion would have been aroused had the will been found while he was barred from the house. Some grounds had, therefore, to be found to bring about a reconciliation with his uncle. The grounds were a reputed business deal showing a profit of 700 per cent. Memoranda of such a concern were in his possession, in code, but such business existed only in imagination.

PETER GREENWELL: So far an unknown figure, but seems to be bound up in some way with Rawson. Has no proved connection with the Cissing house or with the death of Burstall.

ADDENDUM: Rawson would seem to have a thorough knowledge of electrical experimentation on some unknown scale. This is a definite query for investigation. Rawson has done no work for years, but has lived well, undoubtedly on his wits.

For two hours the pair of Yard men talked over the list, discussing the sidelines emanating from the findings, but without arriving at anything which the Doctor could accept as hard facts. In the afternoon Merry, at the Doctor's suggestion, journeyd up to London. 'We've been away some days, now Jim,' he said. 'One of us ought to check over Wilkin's work. Should you have an opportunity you might see if Jones can find anything about our Mr. Peter Greenwell. So far we know no more about him than that he is a familiar of William Rawson, and that they subsequently quarrelled and parted, at Rawson's suggestion.'

In the evening, with Merry back in London, Doctor Manson settled himself in the library, and with the tabulated facts in front of him brought the resources of his keen and logical brain to the problem. Not that he really required the statements; he had a memory that can best be described as 'photographic'. By that is meant that he possessed the rare gift of being able to take a quick and comprehensive glance at a page, say of a newspaper, and a week later be able to describe it minutely, and remember the contents. The late Lord Northcliffe had the same gift.

The Doctor held, with other deep thinkers, that we never 'forget' anything the knowledge of which has once been assimilated. The knowledge, he holds, is simply stored away in a pigeonhole of the brain, and wants only a given circumstance for it to be produced from its cell. The reader of this book can judge for himself the truth of this by the number of occasions on which he, or she, has failed on demand to recall a name or some happening, only for it to spring suddenly to recollection after the search has been abandoned, and when some connecting link had sent the message to the particular cell containing the knowledge.

He began his analytical examination with the first fact — Eadwin Burstall had died unexpectedly.

Why? . . . There was no doubt whatever in his mind of that fact. Doctor Forrestal had pooh-poohed to Mrs. Brandon that her uncle was in a state of *extremis*. Yet next day he was dead. Had the collapse been due, as Forrestal and Sir Charles Hurley had postulated, to the sudden collapse which, according to them, afflicted old men when they were laid low?

With this, the Doctor bracketed in his reasoning the intent — for at one time it was an intent — of Mrs. Brandon to get rid of her uncle and so inherit the estate; and the forged will by which Rawson sought to inherit. It would be a remarkable coincidence, he reasoned, if the death of Burstall had occurred from natural causes at this psychological moment. He did not believe in coincidences of that kind, though he was prepared to admit that truth is sometimes stranger than fiction.

Assuming, therefore, that death was not

natural, who could have pushed the old man off the coil? The answer could only be someone who must have been in close association. Viewing the dossiers as a whole, he came to the decision that the most likely candidate for the dock was Rawson. He, therefore, turned his mind on the nephew. The man's background was a fertile soil in which violence might well grow. He was, the Doctor argued, clearly a crook by desire and practice; his racing career and car career was proof of that. The root of his trouble had been the desire for money; and money had at last come to him through the forged will of Burstall, which was another example of his crookedness. All this hung together and Doctor Manson knew that but for one thing the case would be easy of solution.

That one obstacle, however, was one which seemed to be insoluble — the manner of the death of Eadwin Burstall. No magistrate would send William Rawson for trial on a charge of killing Burstall in the face of the medical evidence that would be called by the defence, even if the Director of Public Prosecutions could be induced by argument and the forged will, to undertake such a prosecution. And no jury would convict on the evidence. Yet, the scientist was convinced in his own mind that all the essentials were in the evidence he had gathered, and that it all came together in a perfect pattern could he but find the key-piece.

Why should Rawson forge a will unless he was determined to benefit from it? Doctor Manson set about arguing against himself. 'Well,' he said to himself, 'he might have forged the will and waited for Burstall to die naturally, the man being old and ill. But (said Manson the detective) when he came to the house with the forged will, or to forge it, he did not know his uncle was ill; he had had no communication with the household since he had been turned out. And, in any case, having forged the will and planted it, why should he stay there? His work was done.'

Again, his bogus business deal was being maintained right up to the moment when Burstall died. Why worry about that after it had served its purpose of getting him back into uncle's favour? Did he stay to ensure that he could bring about the death of his uncle, and then safely plant the forged will? Was there any way in which he could encompass the death without leaving any trace?

The A.C. had referred to the possibility of some secret poison which left no trace. This was, of course, a popular trick of detective writers, when they pulled one out of the hat to confound their readers. As a scientist, Doctor Manson had discounted it, but not ignored it completely. However, all his study of poisons and his arguments with pathologists and toxicologists, including 'Stiffy' Abigail, had resulted in the certainty that there was no poison known to Science that could not leave *some* trace of its existence, had it been used to bring about death.

Was there, then, any other means of killing without leaving trace? In an attempt to find a reply to this postulation Doctor Manson probed minutely into what he knew of the habits of Burstall and Rawson during their cohabitation at 'Hengeclif'. The fact that they became inseparable provided a good starting point. He went over the items he had gleaned concerning that association.

It was, he realised, most noticeable at night. That was agreed. Mrs. Brandon had said that after dinner they spent all the time together in the library drinking whisky. Burstall went to bed at midnight but his nephew remained in the library until the small hours, engaged, he said, on their business. That would be the time when, freed from any interruption either by Burstall or his cousin Aelthea, he could have engaged on the delicate task of altering the first will of Burstall, Manson said to himself. It must have been a great relief to him when he came across the copy of the old will; it saved him from having to forge a completely new document, thereby running the grave risk of being questioned, even by the old and unsuspecting eyes of the old lawyer, Swinburne. It also gave him absolutely genuine signatures of his uncle and two witnesses.

The Doctor wended a way through the maze of this idea, but eventually had to surrender. 'There seems nothing to take hold of in that,' he said to himself. The two men were drinking the same whisky together. Both were heavy drinkers — Burstall all his long life, and Rawson, a man-about-town was known for his convivial habits.

Had Rawson brought about Burstall's death by encouraging him to drink heavily when Doctor Forrestal had advised him against over-indulgence? There was an idea in that except for the fact that whisky was almost second nature to the old man and he (Doctor Manson) knew no precedent for whisky causing, firstly, low blood pressure and, secondly, respiratory weakness, or for aggravating such conditions, if they previously existed, into collapse and death.

It was while he was turning over in his mind this new viewpoint that there came to him that physical curiosity he called his sixth sense. Quite early in his career as an investigator, even when it was amateur scientific investigation before he became mixed up with Scotland Yard, there had been occasions when, puzzling over a problem, he found his pulse beating almost painfully in his left wrist and transmitting a throbbing to the main artery in his neck. It had first alarmed him so considerably that he had consulted his medical adviser. The resultant examination found no reason for the experience. Subsequently, following the line of examination upon which he had been engaged at the time that the experience struck him, it led to a satisfactory conclusion.

When the same feeling assailed him a second time, in a second case, he followed the line of thought deliberately, and again it turned a seeming failure into success. Since then in almost every investigation that troubled him he had worked on, waiting when the problem seemed insoluble for the 'pumping' to indicate that he was on the right track. He likened the emotion to the superstitious powers believed to be invested in a seventh son of a seventh son. Now, with the beating in his neck again throbbing uncomfortably he knew that a thought had come into his mind and was signalling its importance.

Of what had he been thinking? He cast his mind back into the track of thought preceding the experience. A secret poison ... Rawson and Burstall drinking together ... Burstall accustomed to drinking whisky ... what thoughts had come after that?

Suddenly realisation came. He turned back to the notes he had made of his interview with Mrs. Brandon in New York; and the beating crescendoed. He kept his mind going round and round the conviviality of the two men, and ...

Then it came.

There *was* a variation in the men's drinking. There *was* a difference and he like a fool had attached no importance to it when Mrs. Brandon had spoken of it in New York. Note: the reader is given the clue on page (211). Doctor Manson, playing his sixth sense, rang the bell for the housekeeper. When she entered the room he was lying back deep in thought.

She called him back to outside consciousness with a cough. 'Did you want me, sir?'

'Oh, yes, Esther. Do you know where Mr. Burstall obtained his medical waters?' Mrs. Brandon said he used to have a supply and that it did him good. 'I thought I should like some of the same sort. Vasey Water, wasn't it?'

'As to that I don't know, sir. It used to come by the case, but I don't remember the name. But there are still a few bottles in the wine cellar, if you'd like it.'

Doctor Manson gave thanks to his lucky stars. 'That would be very acceptable, Esther. Perhaps you would bring me up a couple of bottles.'

The scientist waited until she had placed a tray with the bottles and a tumbler, and left the room. Then he lifted one of the bottles. It was a half-pint size and around it ran a yellow label with the inscription. 'Vasey Water'. There was no name of maker or distributor on the label, but under the bottom of the bottle was the impress 'W. and A., (Medicinal Waters) Ltd., Harrow'. The water was clear and colourless. The Doctor released a little of the contents into the glass. From a wallet taken from a pocket he extracted a piece of litmus paper and spilt a drop of the liquid in the centre of it. There was no visible change in the litmus. He raised his brows in surprise.

'Decidedly queer,' he muttered to himself. Examination of the litmus paper through a lens seemed to afford him no satisfaction; and accordingly he lifted the glass and drew a little of the liquid into his mouth, rolling it round his palate and then swallowing it. He repeated the performance with a second mouthful.

Now, surprise *did* show in his face, and in his voice. 'It gets curiouser and curiouser,' he said. 'If it's not plain water I'm a Dutchman. Now, what in Heaven's name is the idea of sending out plain water and calling it Vasey Medicinal water? It smacks of another of Rawson's get-rich-quick schemes. At once the mysterious business and the list of figures found in Rawson's writing desk sprang to mind. Was this the 700 per cent profit-making concern? To sell bottles of plain water at a trade price would, indeed, show something like that percentage of profit.

But surely, there was a snag about it. If Eadwin Burstall knew the trick, he surely *would not buy the water and drink it*! It did not ring true. But what other explanation was there? Doctor Manson considered it in silence, seeking some new angle that would satisfactorily explain the seeming absurdity. The throbbing was still perceptible in his neck and wrist.

After two or three minutes of profitless thinking he came to a decision. He lifted the Box of Tricks from its resting place in the bottom bookshelf and, taking from it a Bunsen Burner, a couple of beakers and evaporating apparatus, set them up on the tray on which Esther had brought the bottles.

Half the contents of one bottle he poured into the first of the beakers, set the apparatus up and lit the Bunsen. The reason for the operation will be obvious to any scientist or analytical chemist; should there be any foreign unvolatile substance in the water evaporation would leave behind a substance or sediment which could be identified by microscopic examination. His experiment in the library was, the Doctor knew, a more or less crude affair; but having got the apparatus working, he sat back in his chair, his eyes fixed on the water and the thermometer.

It was some minutes later that he uttered a sharp exclamation, and leaned forward. He stared at the thermometer. It registered one hundred degrees Centigrade. This in itself was not surprising for the Bunsen was burning and it should obviously heat the water in the beaker, while the longer it remained in operation the higher would rise the temperature of the contents.

What was surprising to Doctor Manson was that there was no sign of the water boiling, whereas with the thermometer showing one hundred degrees Centigrade *it should be boiling*. Seconds passed, and still the Doctor sat watching. The first bubble of boiling came with the gauge showing over one hundred and one degrees. The invisible steam poured into the evaporation tube to condense, first into mist and then to liquid, which dripped into the beaker on the opposite side from the Bunsen.

He turned the Bunsen off and left the apparatus to cool. From the Box of Tricks he lifted a table of the boiling points of liquid until he came to a certain item. He closed the book with a snap, and looked at his watch. It showed 7.30 p.m. Picking up his telephone receiver he said: 'This is high priority from Scotland Yard. I want Trinity College, Cambridge, as quickly as you can get it.'

'I'll ring you back, sir,' said the supervisor.

The Doctor sat back, impatiently. The ring came within a few minutes. 'You're through,' the switchboard said.

'Trinity? . . . Doctor Manson here. Put me through to Professor Ballantyne. Should he not be in his room, please find him for me.'

After a brief wait a voice came gruffly over the wire: 'Manson? Ballantyne here . . . You want me?'

'Listen, Ballantyne . . . ' said the Doctor. For three or four minutes he spoke rapidly to the great chemist: and then waited anxiously for the reply.

'Good heavens, Manson what *are* you telling me?' The chemist spoke quietly, but sounded excited. 'But . . . this is *amazing*. I've never heard of such a thing. You're certain, of course . . . yes, it most surely could be so.'

'What would be the most likely symptoms, Ballantyne?' He listened to the reply from Trinity: then responded, 'They are precisely the same as my own set. Thanks. I'll come along in a day or two and tell you all about it.' He replaced the receiver and stared at his own reflection in the mirror over the mantelpiece of the library.

'*My God*,' he said, softly but jubilantly. '*My God, so that's it.*' He went to bed.

17

With his case proved to his own mind, Doctor Manson set himself the task of proving it to the satisfaction of a judge and jury. With the coming of the morning he packed himself, a cardboard box and the Box of Tricks into his big Rolls and set off *en route* for London.

The long, sleek high-powered car ate up the miles through Steyning and Ashington to Horsham, through Leatherhead into Kingston. He then turned off the main track and pushed through Acton and Ealing, and passing Wembley found himself in Harrow. Consulting a local map pasted on the town hall, he turned into a side street beyond Harrow school and found himself pulling up outside the factory of W. & A. (Medicinal Waters) Ltd.

In the office he sent in his card, sealed in one of the firm's envelopes, to the managing director, and a few minutes later was shown into his office, to confront a man eyeing the card, and stroking his moustache in worried mien.

'Good morning, Commander,' the director greeted 'It's a bit of a shock being called on by a Scotland Yard officer. Nothing wrong, I hope?' He looked as though he expected there was.

Now what has the firm been doing under the rose, I wonder, Manson said to himself. Aloud, he replied: 'Nothing that I know of that will land you in my official arms, Mr . . . ?'

'Hartman is the name, sir. I'm glad to be assured of that, anyway. We've been having a spot of bother with one or two orders lately. Well, what can I do for you?'

'What do you make here, Mr. Hartman?' The Doctor hurried on before the director could reply. 'I know, of course, that you manufacture medicinal waters. What I mean is what kind of medicinal water *do* you manufacture?'

'Rather a large order, Commander.' Mr. Hartman's worried look returned. 'Has anyone been complaining of the contents?'

Manson chuckled to himself. So that's the worry, is it? he thought, mentally. Somebody rumbling the racket. He said nothing, but waited. Mr. Hartman after a pause during which he saw that his curiosity was not going to be satisfied, at least at this stage, continued. 'Our manufactures are in pretty considerable variety, sir,' he said. 'For instance there is an iron mixture which is sold as tonic water. Then, there is another of grapefruit and several additional ingredients which are our trade secret. A third to counteract rheumatism contains a certain amount of iodine, another with blended salts is a gentle purgative, and . . . '

Doctor Manson stopped the catalogue with a laugh. 'Hold . . . enough, Mr. Hartman,' he pleaded. 'Of what is your Vasey Water composed?'

Mr. Hartman scratched his head and gaped. 'Our *what?*' he demanded.

'Your Vasey Water.'

'V . . . Va . . . Vasey . . . W . . . Water. Never heard of it. What an appalling name. Why do you think *we* manufacture it?'

Without reply the Doctor opened the cardboard box he had carried from the car and produced one of the bottles from Eadwin Burstall's cellar. He handed it over to the director.

'God bless my soul!' exclaimed Mr. Hartman. His voice was of a timbre that suggested he was shocked to the depths of his soul as by some apparition. 'God bless my soul!' he said again: and rang his desk bell. 'Send Mr. James to me,' he ordered the clerk who answered. 'Mr. James is our works manager,' he explained.

Mr. James, a small nervous man, and who presented the appearance of one who touched nothing in liquid form except the properties of W. & A. (Medicinal Waters) Ltd., crept over to the desk. 'You wanted me, Mr. Hartman?' he asked.

'James, look at that,' roared Mr. Hartman handing over the bottle.

Mr. James took a look at the gaudy mustard-coloured label, and . . .

'Hi! Don't drop the damned thing,' roared Mr. Hartman; and the manager took a firmer grip on the base of the bottle which was about to slip through his hands. 'This gentleman wants to know if we make this appalling looking stuff,' he explained.

Had Mr. James been arraigned before the Holy Office on a charge of blasphemy, he could hardly have looked more horrified. 'Make this . . . *US?*' he asked in a tremulous voice. 'We couldn't make this.' He turned to the Doctor. 'We are very high-class manufacturers of medicinal waters greatly recommended by the medical profession,' he said, 'and the artistry of our labels is one of our recommendations in any shop of repute. This is . . . '

'All right, James, you can go,' ordered Mr. Hartman. He waited until the door had closed. 'There you are, Commander,' he insisted. 'That should satisfy you.' He looked his curiosity. 'What made you think it was one of our commodities?'

Doctor Manson turned the bottle upside down, and exhibited the base to the manufacturer. 'That is your name, is it not?'

'Dammit, so it is.' He took the bottle

and examined it more closely. 'It is definitely one of our bottles, but the stopper is not one of ours; we use a clip-on tin stopper. I can assure you this stuff did not come from our place with the contents that are here.'

'No, I can well believe that, Mr. Hartman,' agreed the Doctor with a chuckle. 'The drinker would want a deuce of a lot of other concoctions if it did. What is intriguing me is how your bottle comes to be used for the mixture inside?'

'Well, sir, that is not a difficult question to answer. Anyone can buy a bottle of any of our preparations. They receive a penny if the bottle is returned to the shop at which they purchased it, but there is no liability on their part to return it. Thus, it is a simple matter to put something else in the bottle and cork it.'

'Quite so. I can understand that in a single bottle, Mr. Hartman. But in this instance I have cases of the bottles, all labelled like this, and all bearing your imprint on the base. And to the best of my belief there have been others.'

The director looked up, startled. 'The

devil you have,' he said. 'Come and have a word with our bottling manager.' He led the way to an office at the back of the yard and called over a sturdy young man wearing a baize apron. Mr. Hartman explained to him the circumstances, and the man examined the bottle. He turned it round and round and then, after a closer look, held it up to the light.

'As a matter of fact, sir, I can tell you near enough the date at which it left us.' he said. 'It is one of a consignment which was a little lighter in colour than usual. And I complained to the makers because it was too clear and made the contents look too much like clear water. I overcame the difficulty by using the consignment for the grape juice cordial. That preparation has a slight green tinge,' he explained for the benefit of Doctor Manson, 'so the clearness did not matter a great deal.'

'That is an exceedingly good and useful point, and does credit to your powers of observation,' said Doctor Manson. 'Can you tell me whether you have ever sent a supply of your waters to a Mr. William

Rawson at an address in the Edgware Road?'

The man looked up his book. 'No, sir,' he said. 'We have had no orders from anyone of that name.'

'Do you deliver anywhere in the Edgware Road?' The Doctor persisted.

'We have a regular order from Messrs. Wildruff, a firm of grocers there, sir.'

'Whereabouts in the Edgware Road are they situated?'

'That I don't know, but . . . ' He looked outside at a line of vans drawn up. 'Ah, Bill Camplin is there. He'll know because he delivers in that area. Hi, Bill,' he called, and one of the men looked round. 'Whereabouts is Wildruff's in the Edgware Road?'

'Right bang in front of John's Wood Road at the corner of the street opposite,' came the reply.

'Fine,' enthused Doctor Manson. 'Then I think that is all.' He accompanied Mr. Hartman back to the office.

'I hope you are satisfied that we know nothing of the stuff you've brought, Commander,' Hartman said.

'Quite satisfied. I never had any doubt about it, but I wanted to learn if you could tell me anything that might help. You have done so.'

'Anything badly wrong?'

'There is, but it is nothing in which your name or your goods will be mentioned. Many thanks for your help.'

The director breathed a sigh of relief; and Doctor Manson, re-entering his car, continued on his way to Scotland Yard. At the C.I.D. headquarters he parked the Rolls in its accustomed place, and climbed the stairs to the laboratory on the top floor of the building. Merry working at a test bench, looked up as the door opened. His eyes roved for a moment over the face of his chief. Then he stood bolt upright.

'You've got it, Harry!' he said with complete conviction. The two had worked together on crime investigation for years and the Deputy Scientist knew every facet of Manson's character and demeanour, and he read his face like a book.

The Doctor answered with a slow

smile, and the satisfaction of the successful hunter was in his voice as he answered: 'Yes, I have it, Jim.'

'What is it?'

For reply the Doctor lifted two bottles out of the cardboard box and placed them on the table near the microscope on which his deputy was working. 'Go into these, Jim,' he said. 'Try boiling a little of the contents, then weigh a little and try it under the microscope. Then tell me what you think.'

While his deputy got down to the task, Doctor Manson sat down at his desk and wrote rapidly in his notebook, afterwards copying his report on to a sheet of foolscap paper. This, when completed, he slipped into an inner pocket. Merry crossed over to him, a smile in his eyes and confidence in his demeanour.

'Well?' asked Manson.

'Boils at 101.4 deg. C. Maximum density at 11.6 C. There is no doubt at all what it is, but what does it do, Harry?'

'Well, Jim, Ballantyne said . . . ' He gave his deputy the gist of the conversation he had had with the Cambridge professor the evening before. 'It coincides entirely with my own opinion,' he said. 'I am going to Trinity to see Ballantyne and go into the points at greater lengths, and in more confined scientific detail. Meanwhile, I'll go and surprise the A.C.' He left the laboratory, and made his way down the staircase to the first floor. There he walked along a corridor until he reached a door midway along. He stepped through it.

'Sir Edward in, Mildmay?' he asked of the sergeant at a desk.

'Yes, Doctor, and he's alone,' was the reply.

The Doctor opened the inner door and entered the room of the Assistant Commissioner (C) — the 'C' being for 'Crime'. Sir Edward looked up. 'Hallo, Harry. Didn't know you were back in town. I want someone to talk to, so it's lucky you dropped in. Had a bit of wigging from the Home Secretary about what he calls lack of crime prevention. It appears he's being chased by a few M.P.s whose constituents want to know for what we pay a police rate. Sit down, and have a cigar.'

Doctor Manson took a seat. He selected a cigar from the box of Coronas offered him, removed the band, and lit the weed. He blew a smoke ring towards the ceiling.

Then, casually as though he was merely passing the time of day, he said:

'*I know, Edward, how Eadwin Burstall was killed.*'

18

The right hand of Sir Edward Allen which was lifting a cigar to his lips, stayed its course. His eyes stared, puzzled, at the scientist in much the same mesmerised way as a rabbit faces the cold, unblinking stare of the serpent for whom it is destined as a meal. For a minute — a long minute to Sir Edward — he presented the appearance of one of those tableaux which the music hall audiences of long ago watched with bated breath. Then came the change for which those same audiences waited. The A.C. moved. He bent forward, and his fingers laid the cigar carefully in an ashtray in front of him; and he spoke:

'Harry, I thought you said that you knew how Eadwin Burstall was *murdered*,' he begged.

Doctor Manson took his cigar between his fingers and waggled it in front of the A.C.

'I *did* say that, Edward — that Burstall *was murdered*. I've said it from the first, you know . . . '

'But couldn't prove it.'

'No. But *now I know how he was killed*. It is a method, I may say, entirely new in homicide.'

'By Rawson?' the A.C. asked.

The Doctor considered before he replied. When he spoke it was in guarded words. 'I will go only so far as to say that I know of nobody but Rawson who is involved. Beyond that I will not go until I have more facts on which to base a definite opinion.'

'Is this an outcome of your . . . '

'Of my suspicious mind, you were going to say,' the scientist interrupted. 'O, ye of little faith, Edward.' He eyed his chief in sorrow. 'Be not faithless, but believing,' he quoted. 'No, it is not my suspicious mind. At least, it started with my suspicious mind, but it was finally settled by good honest-to-goodness scientific evidence which I can put in front of the Director of Public Prosecutions and a judge and jury.'

He extracted from his inside pocket the foolscap sheet which he had filled with writing while waiting the outcome of Merry's final test in the laboratory.'

'That's it,' he said, and passed it over.

Five minutes passed before the A.C. laid the document on his desk and turned towards his friend and chief investigator. 'Masterly,' he said. 'Incredible! The best piece of work you've done since you joined us. What a plot! What a . . . ' He sidetracked further encomiums. 'What are you going to do next?'

'I think we ought to get that apparatus from Rawson before anything leaks out, or before he himself moves it. I think there is still enough in it to make a test, now that we know what to look for. I suggest that Jones, Kenway and I go down with a couple of men and one of our vans and bring it here. Then we shall have to get hold of Rawson. We'll have to entice him in some way outside the boundaries of Monte Carlo, because we can't take him from inside there, you know.'

'Is that going to be difficult, Harry?'

'I don't think so. It's a curious place is

the Principality. Half the place is under the jurisdiction of the French authorities, and one or two of the hotels and night spots come in the French part. We can probably entice him into one of them, or wait for him to appear there through some other, and more pleasant, source of enticement.'

'*Cherchez la femme*, I suppose?'

'Possibly, Edward. Will you get me a search warrant for Rawson's flat?'

The A.C. eyed him accusingly. 'Did you have one when you went there the last time?' he demanded.

'I . . . er . . . rather think Mrs. Biggs the landlady invited us in, Edward,' Manson replied.

Sir Edward shook his head. 'All very irregular,' he said, reprovingly, but without much sting. 'The Home Secretary would have the coat off my back if he knew about it. I'll get the warrant.'

Fortuitous circumstances, however, relieved them of the task of chasing Rawson through the hidden purlieus of Monte Carlo. The Doctor, Superintendent Jones and Chief-Inspector Kenway, armed with the necessary warrant, drove to the house in Edgware Road. When the inspector's ring was answered by Mrs. Biggs, he put the formal question for such occasions:

'Is Mr. William Rawson at home, please?'

To the complete astonishment of the three officers, the woman replied in the affirmative. 'He's upstairs in his flat, gentlemen,' she announced. 'What name shall I say?'

'Never mind, madam, we'll go right up.' Superintendent Jones gave the answer and stepped through the doorway. With Inspector Kenway leading they mounted to the top floor and knocked on the door of the flat.

'Mr. William Rawson?' asked the inspector of the man who opened the door.

'That's me. But I don't know you. How did you get up here without my being told there were callers. I have told Mrs. Biggs . . . '

'Don't blame Mrs. Biggs, sir. We walked up. We are police officers and want a few minutes' talk with you.' He stepped into the room followed by the others.

In the sitting-room Rawson faced his visitors. They noticed no sign of perturbation in his face or demeanour. 'Now, what do you want?' he demanded. 'I have to see my solicitor in half an hour.'

Superintendent Jones glanced at Doctor Manson and received a confirmatory nod. He stepped forward. 'I am Chief Superintendent Jones of Scotland Yard, Mr. Rawson, and these gentlemen are Commander Doctor Manson of the C.I.D. and Detective Chief Inspector Kenway, also of the C.I.D. I believe you are Mr. William Rawson, nephew of Mr. Eadwin Burstall, of Cissing, in the county of Sussex?'

'Quite correct. Only you should have said the late Mr. Eadwin Burstall. He is dead.'

'Just so,' agreed the superintendent, 'and you have inherited his estate under his will?'

'As to that, sir, shall I say I am heir to the estate. I have received damn little money so far, thanks to the lawyers. That is what I am going to see them about today.'

Doctor Manson took up the questioning. 'Before Mr. Burstall's death, Mr. Rawson, he was associated with you in some sort of business, I understand. What was the nature of the undertaking in which you were partners?'

'What the devil business is that of the police? I've nothing to say. It's a piece of dashed impertinence,' he blustered. 'The business was a distinctly private matter between by uncle and myself.'

Doctor Manson ignored the bluster; he detected behind it a certain strain in the man. But he showed no sign of his thought, and continued quietly with his questions. 'A private matter between you and your uncle, Mr. Rawson? But your uncle is dead, and the estate has to be proved, you know. Certain sums of money passed between your uncle and you, apparently in connection with this business. They have to be accounted for. And so have any profits due to the estate from the business company.' He paused for a reply from Rawson. None was forthcoming: and the Doctor continued:

'Inquiries have failed to reveal that you have ever been engaged in any company in which Mr. Burstall may conceivably have been partner or a shareholder. Would you like to tell me what was the nature of this business, and what transactions were carried out?'

'I have already said that the business was a private matter between my uncle and me.'

'I see,' Doctor Manson said. He turned to Superintendent Jones. 'I think he should be warned before we go any further,' he suggested. The superintendent looked across at Inspector Kenway: and the inspector stepped forward. 'William Rawson,' he said. 'You know who I am, and you know that these gentlemen are police officers. I have to warn you that you are not bound to answer any questions, or to make any statement, but whatever you do say will be taken down in writing and may be used in evidence. Do you understand that; and do you wish to make a statement?' He looked at the Doctor.

'Rawson,' Manson said, and the man turned to face him. 'If I suggested that there was never any business, but that you used some hypothetical profit-making transaction to gain re-entry into the house of your uncle, from which you had been barred, in order to ingratiate your self into his good opinion and in order to obtain money from him, what would you say to that? You have heard that you need not make any reply unless you desire to do so. Is there anything you would like to say?'

Rawson looked from one to another of his inquisitors. He thought for a few moments, and then to the surprise of the three sat down and laughed.

'All right . . . you win,' he said. 'There never was any business. It was, as you say, a ruse to get into uncle's good graces. I knew, knowing nunky, that a nice bit of profit in the offing would do the trick. Gawd, I knew him all right. It did. He jumped at a nice fat profit which anybody but uncle would have realised couldn't have been earned. And

I wanted capital.

'But he never gave me any money for the business. You're wrong there, laddie. He gave it to me for my pocket until I had the business on a firm footing. Then he was coming into it with capital.'

'Pity . . . you . . . didn't . . . tell . . . that at first, ain't it?' Jones said.

Doctor Manson had walked through the flat to the kitchen, and now called from there: 'What is in this cupboard, Rawson?' he asked.

'Only a bit of machinery,' was the reply. On the invitation of the scientist, he opened it. Superintendent Jones, who was seeing it for the first time, probed it ocularly.

'Is this yours?'

'It is, I bought it, if you want to know.'

'Do you use it?'

'Well, sir, what do you suppose I bought it for.'

'A still of some kind, isn't it?'

'Yes, it is a still.'

'Like to tell us for what purpose you bought it?'

'No. I don't see why I should. I have

not broken the law. I bought it second-hand.'

Doctor Manson came to a sudden decision. 'I am going to detain you for further questioning, Rawson,' he said. 'I think it will be better for it to take place in Scotland Yard, and I am proposing to have this machinery moved there as well.'

At Central Office, Rawson was accommodated in the office of Chief Detective Inspector Kenway, while the scientist and Merry were busy in the laboratory with the vacuum still. Some time was necessary to identify the little amount of liquid in the apparatus with the liquid contained in the bottles in the cellar of the late Mr. Burstall. When the analysis was complete Doctor Manson and Superintendent Jones, accompanied by the Assistant Commissioner (C) himself, crowded the room of the inspector. Rawson stood up in alarm at the invasion.

'William Rawson,' began the Doctor, 'you have already been warned that you need not make any statement, but I am warning you again in order that there can be no mistake about it. In reply to questions asked you in your flat, you stated that you invented a story of a business in order to ingratiate yourself into your uncle's good graces. I am now going to suggest to you that that story is a tissue of lies; that it was not with the intention of getting into your uncle's good graces that you got into his house under guise of this business, but that you went there for the purpose of forging, or having forged, of leaving to be discovered the will under which you are named as the heir to your uncle's estate. That will has been proved to be a forgery. Inspector Kenway will read the charge over to you.'

The Doctor waited until the formal charge had been read out, then: 'I think you should know that in view of what I am going to say, you are entitled to ask for the presence of a solicitor. In fact, in my view it is most desirable that a lawyer should be present. Is there any particular one you would like us to send for?'

Rawson swallowed hard, and the Adam's Apple in his throat worked convulsively up and down. 'Young Butterworth,' he said almost in a whisper.

'Freddie Butterworth . . . know him?'

It was a quarter-of-an-hour later that the lawyer was ushered into the room. He looked round the company, nodded to the A.C. and crossed to Rawson. 'What's it all about, Bill?' he asked.

The A.C. answered. 'Perhaps I had better tell you, Butterworth,' he said: and gave a *précis* of the interrogation so far.

'And you are charging my client with forgery?' He looked from one to the other. 'Are you detaining him now?'

The A.C. nodded.

'Then we have nothing to say at this stage,' the lawyer announced.

'There is still another charge,' Doctor Manson said, quietly.

'Another! What?'

'The late Eadwin Burstall did not die a natural death. We are charging Rawson with the wilful murder of his uncle.' Doctor Manson produced the warrant.

'Oh, my God!' said Butterworth, but his words were drowned by a scream from Rawson. 'No, no!' he screamed. 'No! It's a lie. I didn't. I never did, I tell you. I admit the forgery. I'll plead guilty to that.

But I didn't kill the old man.' He looked at the lawyer. 'You know that, Freddie. I'd never have the pluck.' He raised his voice again. 'I'll tell you about the will. I'll . . . ' His voice died away from sheer mental exhaustion.

The A.C. looked questioningly at the lawyer. 'What do you say to that, Butterworth?' he asked. 'Do you want him to make a statement?'

'If he makes a statement, I suppose you will question him on it?'

The A.C. nodded gravely. 'It is, as you know, customary, Butterworth.'

'Then I think I will advise him to make a statement. I believe what he says when he states that he would never have the pluck to commit murder, or even try it. I've known him for a long time. We'll make a statement, provided I can object to any question, an answer to which I think could incriminate him.'

'Agreed,' said the A.C.

'It is true that I forged a will leaving my uncle's estate to me,' Rawson said beginning his statement. 'I first thought of it last year. I was in a bad way for money.

I had been living pretty high and was down to nearly my last penny. Also, I had borrowed on the security of my uncle's legacy under the will of which he had told Aelthea and me. The man was pressing me for repayment, and said he would go to my uncle for the money. He did not know I had been turned out by uncle. I told him that if he went to uncle he would ruin me, uncle wouldn't pay him and he'd get no money at all. But I knew I had to have money. I knew I would have to get into uncle's house in order to plant the will if I forged it . . . '

'Just a minute, Rawson,' said Doctor Manson. 'Did you conceive this forgery yourself, or was it put into your head?'

'A friend suggested to me that a forged will would enable me to borrow on the strength of it,' Rawson said. 'I thought for a long time on how I could get back into 'Hengeclif',' he went on. 'Then I decided that if I posed as having made good, and went to him with a business proposition which would show big profits, I could get away with it for a time, and give me a chance to put the will somewhere where

287

it would be found. Well, you know that I got in all right. I had uncle's signature on the letter he wrote to me inviting me to let him see the business proposition, but I had to be sure that it was his real signature . . .'

'Because you thought he might have written a little differently, since you had been in the forgery line before, Rawson?' suggested the Assistant Commissioner.

Rawson gulped. 'Who told you that?' he asked. 'Anyway, what does it matter? I typed a new will and wrote his signature. But I didn't think it was very good, and I couldn't get uncle's queer phrasing very well. It didn't seem quite all right to me, but it was the best I could do, and I worked out that uncle would be dead by the time it came to be read, and couldn't dispute it.

'Then, one night, after we had talked over the business deal and uncle had gone to bed very drunk, I was going through his desk when I came across the old will which he'd cancelled and in which the estate was divided equally between Aelthea and me. It was all in uncle's writing and was witnessed, and I saw that if I was careful, I could change two parts of it. I got a book all about inks and what to do to make ink look a different colour, and I tried all kinds of ways. It took me a month to get the will right.'

Some queer instinct made him turn towards Doctor Manson. 'How did you find out that it was a forgery?' he asked.

The scientist smiled slightly. 'You left many clues behind, Rawson. For instance, the acid you used to remove the original writing left a slight yellow stain, not visible to unaided eyesight, but distinguishable when photographed with a filter in front of the camera lens. Then, although you allowed the ink you used to stay exposed to the air, and mixed it with coffee to give it the required colour, you used a different kind of ink from that in your uncle's ink-bottle. And finally, you wrote with a gold nib, whereas your uncle did not use a fountain-pen. All this was perfectly plain to us after we had arrived at the first suspicion.'

'I see,' said Rawson, mournfully. 'I wasn't clever enough to get away with it.'

'It was, if I may say so, an excellent effort, Rawson,' said Doctor Manson. 'Except for one thing, it would never have been suspected and therefore never investigated. I was in the house on holiday, without any suspicion of any untoward happening. Mr. Burstall, I was told, had died a natural death.'

'My God!' came from Rawson. 'What was the one thing, sir?'

'You left your book on inks in the bookcase. There was no other book on scientific science in the library. I took it out, and the passages you had marked in the book excited my curiosity. But go on with your statement, and don't ask questions.'

'Soon after I had finished the will, uncle became very ill, and I could tell after the London specialist had been, that he wouldn't live long. So I stayed on. When uncle died, I slipped the will among the papers in the back of his desk. I knew it must be found, but was afraid Aelthea would find and destroy it when she saw what it said. I was dumbfounded when old Swinburne read out another will. So I was glad when, after that, Swinburne said he wanted to go through uncle's papers. Then, when he found the will and said it was genuine, I thought I was safe.

'I didn't kill my uncle. Why it's madness to think I did. I knew he was dying and I could wait. Besides, I've said I wouldn't have the pluck to do it. I had thought if it was possible to do it by poison. Only I read that it was impossible not to detect poison in the body of a person.'

He ceased, took a deep breath. 'That's all I can say.'

He ceased speaking and sat back in his chair. Moisture was standing in beads on his forehead. He looked anxiously at Manson. The Doctor moved his chair so that it gave him a clear view of the man's face. 'Rawson,' he said, 'the will you had forged was no good, of course, until your uncle was dead. You had no real business and you knew that your uncle, who was no fool, would be bound to discover that before long. Then he would turn you out — and for good. *Is it not strange that he should have died so soon after you had* completed the forgery?'

'No, sir. I have said that I knew he was dying.'

'*You knew nothing of the sort,*' the scientist rapped out. '*When you first thought of forging the will, and when you were doing it in that very house, Eadwin Burstall was in perfectly good health. His health did not begin to decline until after you appeared there.* Doctor Forrestal was not called in until after you had been there for some weeks. He was taken ill shortly after the will had been forged. Is that not so?'

'You need not answer that question,' the lawyer advised. 'Men have to start being ill some time, Doctor,' he added.

'Just as you like,' replied the Doctor. He turned again to Rawson. 'You and your uncle did a lot of drinking at night, did you not?'

'We drank a bit, yes.'

'What did you drink?'

'Whisky.'

'Did you drink it neat?'

'No. Uncle had water with his. I had ginger-ale.'

'Why did you not have water, Rawson?'

'Because I do not like water with whisky. I always have ginger-ale.'

'Is that the only reason?' He stood up. 'I want to move this conversation to my laboratory, Sir Edward,' he said, and led the way. On the bench under the windows of the laboratory stood the apparatus which had been removed from the Edgware Road flat. Reconstructed and spread out, with the background of the laboratory around it, it presented a formidable piece of experimental machinery. The scientist drew attention to it.

'You recognise this, Rawson?' he asked. 'I think you told me it belonged to you. You bought it second-hand. You said, when I asked you its purpose, that it was your concern. It is now our concern, also. So, how did you use this machine?'

The man twisted in the chair with which he had been provided. He thought for a moment and then said: 'It has nothing to do with uncle's will.'

Doctor Manson, after eyeing him reflectively for a moment seemed with his next question to have left the subject.

'Where did your uncle obtain the special water which he mixed with his whisky?'

'It was a tonic water sent down from London.'

'By you?'

'I took the first few bottles down, and then uncle said he wanted a tonic and told me to get some more. So I ordered a supply every week.'

'Why could you not have ordered it in Cissing, or Worthing?'

'Nobody had heard of it down there. It was a new water and there wasn't much of it being made.'

'Where can I get a supply?'

'You can't sir. It didn't pay and the company stopped it.'

'Were you in this company?'

'I had some money in it — yes.'

'Was the company W. & A. (Medicinal Waters) Ltd?'

'Yes.'

'Would it surprise you to hear that W. & A. have never heard of this concoction?'

Rawson made no reply.

Doctor Manson's face was now set in grave lines. He turned to the solicitor. 'I want to be quite fair to your client, Butterworth,' he said, slowly. 'And I think I will leave you to have a chat with him. I want to tell you that we are going to say that the water of which we are talking caused the death of Eadwin Burstall. I have tested some of the contents of the bottles that were left at 'Hengeclif', and I have also tested some of the dregs of liquid that remained in this machinery when we seized it. The contents are identical. Rawson has said that the still is his, and that he used it. He has also admitted that he had some interest in the water supplied to his uncle. In view of these admissions, and his further admission of having forged a will entirely in his favour, and the fact that his uncle was taken fatally ill shortly afterwards — well, you realise the position in which your client is placed do you not? We'll leave you to talk the position over with him. When you are ready to see us, there will be a constable outside this door.'

It was a quarter-of-an-hour later that Mr. Butterworth poked his head round the door and nodded the company back to his client.

'I think I've got the truth out of this young fool now, Sir Edward,' he announced, addressing the Assistant Commissioner. 'In detail, he says the machine is his, insofar as he paid for it, and claims it. But it was never at any time used by him. He bought it, he says, for a friend who had the idea of making money out of water. He met a man in a club and had the scheme put up to him. It is a shady scheme, which is the reason he did not want to disclose it to you; he has already been deep enough in shady business.

'He understands that a certain amount of a chemical was added to distilled water, which could then be sold very profitably as a mineral water. A costing account was produced by this man, together with an estimated nett profit. All the man wanted was capital to purchase the apparatus for bringing out the first samples of water, and somewhere where he could live. That, Rawson says, he provided in his flat in the Edgware Road.

The understanding was that when he could show that the water was a genuine tonic, a firm would take it over and pay them a handsome sum for the rights.

'Rawson tells me that quite a number of weeks went by and no money was forthcoming although, according to this man, the firm had taken over Vasey Water. The two of them quarrelled over money matters and Rawson turned the man out. Rawson emphatically denies that he had anything to do with the water process, and denies that it was anything but what it purported to be. He took the first supply to Cissing on this man's suggestion; and the only money he ever had out of it was that paid by his uncle for supplies ordered and delivered; and half of that he shared with the man.'

'Was this man a Peter Greenwell?' Doctor Manson asked.

'It was; and I can say here and now that I believe Rawson's story.'

'From the varying stories we have heard, Mr. Butterworth, I should not think Rawson is capable of telling a straight truth,' the A.C. said. 'He seems to tell the truth about one thing only when he is in danger of a worse thing. Can you produce this man Greenwell?'

'We cannot. It appears that after Mr. Burstall's death Greenwell wrote to my client demanding money. He said that he had seen in Rawson's desk in the flat what looked like a will leaving Rawson his uncle's estate. I should say here that Greenwell was the man who had suggested the idea of forging a will. Apparently the document he saw was the typed copy which Rawson has told us he prepared before he found the old will at 'Hengeclif'. Greenwell said the will was obviously forged, and he wanted his share in the money to keep quiet about it. He asked for a reply to be sent c/o the Post Office at Notting Hill Gate. Rawson seems to have shown the only bit of sense in this story by writing to him stating that he had no intention of paying blackmail, and would go to the police.

'Hearing nothing further from Greenwell, he wrote to the post office asking if a letter to Greenwell had been called for and was told that it had. Since then he has neither seen nor heard of Greenwell. By the way, you can test part of this story to some extent by the electricity account for Rawson's flat which became heavy only after the arrival there of Greenwell.'

'That is so,' Doctor Manson said. 'It is within my own knowledge.'

'Had Rawson seen this man prior to the occasion at the club which he mentioned?' the A.C. asked.

Mr. Butterworth looked at his client, who shook his head. 'Never, sir,' said Rawson.

'What club was it?'

'The Nighthawk, sir.'

'Birds . . . of . . . feather . . . flock together,' shot out Superintendent Jones. 'An' . . . good featherin' . . . ground.'

A sharp exclamation came from Doctor Manson and checked further remarks from the superintendent. He turned to Rawson. 'These accounts which Greenwell produced to you — were they those which we found in your desk, and were they also the ones which you used to delude your uncle into believing you had a good business proposition?'

Rawson nodded. 'I thought it *was* good.'

'And you say that Greenwell supplied the water which Doctor Manson has told you caused your uncle's death?' the A.C. demanded.

'If it did cause uncle's death, then it must have been him.'

'You told us that you had never seen Greenwell before the club meeting. Did he know your uncle?'

'I don't suppose so.'

'Now, Rawson, listen to me carefully.' The A.C. fixed his monocle into his perfectly good left eye and stared hard at the man. 'If all this happened as you say, you realise, do you not, that Greenwell must have plotted deliberately to murder your uncle. Now, tell me this: *Why should he want to kill a man that he did not know, and from whom he could gain no financial advantage, and do it through you who, unknown to him at the time, were engaged by forgery in providing a fortune for yourself on your uncle's death?'*

'I don't know sir. I can't think. It

sounds crazy to me that he should think of killing uncle.' His voice broke. 'But everything I have told you is true.'

'Very well. What kind of man was this Greenwell. Describe him to us. Was he tall, or short, stout or thin?'

'He is nearly the same height and size as myself. He had dark hair, but I think it was dyed, because when it grew it looked different.'

'That doesn't help very much. What habits had he? You can tell a man better by his habits.'

'Well, he drank a great deal and he was good company, I gather. Girls we both knew said he spoke very nicely, 'la-di-la' was how they described it. He went down well with them. They said he was court . . . courti . . . '

'Is it courtly you're thinkin' of?' asked Superintendent Jones.

Sir Edward stared at his superintendent in surprise, but recognition appeared in Rawson's face. 'Yes, that's what they called him, a courtier.'

'What did he usually drink?' Jones asked.

'Mostly pink gins.'

Superintendent Jones retired behind the A.C., Doctor Manson and Butterworth. He caught the arm of Kenway, and with a finger pressed to his lips, hustled him noiselessly out of the room. Watched anxiously by Butterworth, and in more or less terror by Rawson, Sir Edward and Doctor Manson held a whispered confabulation; at the end the A.C. addressed the solicitor. 'Well, Butterworth,' he said, 'we feel inclined for the moment not to pursue the more serious charge. That is not to say that we may not prefer it at some future date. Doctor Manson thinks that there are one or two points in your story that cling together and which, if truthful, may put Rawson clear of the murder charge. We will have them more closely investigated, and we will try to find this man Greenwell. But we shall, of course, hold Rawson on his confession of forgery, and we shall oppose bail when he is brought in front of the magistrates. His confession will of course be sent to the solicitors dealing with the Burstall will. Now,

Jones . . . ' The A.C. turned and stopped in the middle of a sentence. 'Where the deuce are Jones and Kenway?' he asked.

'They were here a minute or two ago,' Doctor Manson said. He rang his desk bell. 'Have you seen Superintendent Jones, Snell?' he asked of the sergeant who answered.

'No sir, I thought he was with you.'

'What the devil has happened to the two of them?' asked the Doctor.

'Perhaps your lab. has swallowed them up, Harry,' the A.C. said. 'It does all kinds of queer tricks, you know.'

'Not disappearing ones, Edward. *Ap*-pearing ones, as a rule.'

19

'What the devil is the idea?' Kenway, following Jones at a lurching half-trot, asked the question.

'Gotta hunch,' Jones said.

'Hunch! I reckon we'll get the sack to put it in, too.'

'C'mon in here.' Fat man led the way into the Salisbury Club. 'Up . . . back . . . stairs . . . private . . . room.'

Now, the Salisbury was a club which sought no members; members came only by personal recommendation; and the best qualification was a record card in the files of Scotland Yard. It was, in fact, the recreational *collectanea* of the higher flights of crookdom — the 'con' men, 'Flash' men and swindlers in a big way. In a private room eight men sat round a table at one end of which rested a card 'slipper' or 'shoe'. 'Well, well,' Jones said admiringly. '*Chemin de Fer*, eh? . . . Gotta . . . tak' . . . one o' the players,' he added to the alarmed faces staring at him in dismay. He hooked a finger at the player he had recognised.

'Want . . . you,' he said. 'No . . . arrest mind yer . . . Just . . . little chat . . . you'n me.'

He landed him in the interview room of the Yard and then rejoined the company in the A.C.'s room.

'Dammit, he's reappeared,' the A.C. said. 'Where the . . .'

Jones broke into the sentence with a whisper in the ears of Manson and Sir Edward. Sir Edward scratched his head.

'All right, I'll play along. But why the mystery? What with you dragging strange folks in by the neck with no charge, and the Doctor here walking into people's houses when they aren't there, you'll have me out in the street before you've finished. Where is this friend of ours?'

'In the interview room. I'll be gettin' back there now.'

Sir Edward dialled a number on the house phone. 'Take Rawson to the interview room,' he said. 'Don't go in. Let him look through the one way window and see if he can recognise anybody.'

Rawson looked and was taken back to detention. Sir Edward and Doctor Manson walked down to the interview room and reached it at the precise moment that Superintendent Jones poked his head round the lintel. 'Well?' Fat Man demanded.

'All is well,' Manson said. 'He says it is Greenwell.' A series of rumbling chuckles shook the big form of the superintendent. 'Good Lord, Jones,' said the startled A.C., 'what on earth did you have for lunch? Well, let's have a look at Mr. Greenwell.' The three walked together into the room. Sir Edward stared incredulously.

'Timmins!' he said.

'Timmins,' echoed Jones and the satisfaction in his voice was a joy to hear.

'Gold-darn it,' said Mr. Timmins. 'You ought to know me by now. I'm on regular visiting terms with you . . . aren't I?'

'Quite. But it was the other name that surprised us, Timmins.'

'What other name?'

'Peter Greenwell.'

A look of bewilderment dawned on Timmin's face. 'Who the hell is Peter Greenwell?'

'You,' Jones said.

'Don't let us bandy words,' Doctor Manson said. 'You took physics at Oxford didn't you, Timmins? Come upstairs and I'll show you something that may surprise you even more.' He stood the man in front of the electrolytic apparatus. 'Recognise your old friend?' he asked.

'Perhaps you can tell me what it is, and then I can enjoy the joke with you.'

A ring on the phone interrupted the conversation. 'For me, I think,' Jones said. 'I'll be down.' He did return to the room after a couple of minutes, hiding behind his big form a visitor. 'Who's this, Mrs. Biggs?' he asked and stepped quickly to one side.

Mrs. Biggs who had been snatched from her kitchen and hurried to the Yard in a squad car, looked round the company, and said: 'Why, it's Mr. Greenwell, of course.' — and was escorted out.

'I see. So Rawson split after all, did he.

So! All right, I'm Greenwell. Now I'll say my piece. Rawson forged the will which gave him his uncle's property. I saw . . . '

'We know all that Timmins. And your attempts to blackmail him,' the A.C. said.

'Look,' Manson said. 'Let us keep to Mr. Greenwell rather than his better known self 'Black' Timmins.' He fingered the vacuum still as he spoke. 'What exactly did you produce from this apparatus, Timmins?'

'What do you suppose, Mr. Scientist? *Barley* water?'

'No, not barley water. You left just enough contents — probably unknowingly because you forgot condensation — for me to analyse the contents and compare them with the bottles of 'medicinal' water which went to Eadwin Burstall at Cissing. *And Eadwin Burstall died.*'

For a moment Timmins stood staring . . . staring. Then he raised his arms as though to dive at the man standing in his path, as the figure of Justice stands in the path of the wrongdoer. They stayed raised only for a second or two, before Timmins sank to the ground in collapse. He crumbled as though every bone in his body had suddenly disintegrated, and he lay in a heap.

The last chapter in the life and death of Eadwin Burstall, the ancient Saxon inheritor, had been written.

* * *

'Dammit, Harry, I never knew anything like it,' the A.C. said. 'There wasn't a case for you to investigate, and you were on holiday. There wasn't anything suspicious . . .'

'Only my well-known suspicious mind, eh, Edward? That and people hunting secretly in my library; three sheets of notes on the effects of poison; an unexpected death; and two very odd changes of wills.

'Worked out, the story is really simple. Timmins knew at second hand that Aelthea Whiting was a very old man's heiress because he had heard it from someone who had a gentleman friend in Swinburne's office. He followed up the hint and contrived to meet her when she went on holiday to Brighton, and stayed with her at Rottingdean. He has been described as a courtier, and Miss Whiting fell for him.

'Then she met Brandon, and liked him better. All Timmins could do about that was to blackmail her to keep him quiet. So he turned to the nephew as a second string; one of 'em would land a dollop in any case.

'I think that at first he had some hopes of the tonic water, and thought he might sell the rights to a company. He had cultivated Rawson, as the old man's nephew, and got the use of the flat in Edgware Road. Then it was, I think, that he learned that Rawson had been thrown out by uncle.

'That was a blow. He suggested, I think, that Rawson might get back into grace and favour if he could show the old man a highly paying proposition. As we know it worked, helped by an accountancy he drew up. That was when Timmins thought of the idea of getting rid of Burstall in order that there might be more for him, either through the nephew or by blackmail of the girl. He had read Physics at Oxford, and I am told was a brilliant man at the job. But blackmail of women paid better. He started on the stuff that would, with the help of heavy drinking, kill the old man and release the money bags. That's the whole story.'

'But, Doctor,' burst out Superintendent Jones. 'We've heard all about the stuff that killed the old man. But you've never given it a name. What the hell is it?'

'No more I haven't, Fat Man,' the Doctor said with a smile. 'Well, the stuff, as you call it, is Heavy Water.'

'Heavy Water! . . . Never . . . heered . . . of it.'

'I don't suppose you have. With good reason. It has never been used in murder. The Burstall case makes homicidal history. Even detective writers, who have vivid imaginations, have never thought of it.'

'What the blazes is it, anyway?'

'Perhaps I'd better read you what a very distinguished chemist, a research specialist at the Lyons Institute of Criminology, says of it.' He read ' 'It is agreed that it is toxic. It has the effect of slowing down the metabolism and would cause death among old people with low metabolic activity, if they continually ingested it. It increases the toxity of alcohol with the effect that what in ordinary circumstances could be thought a case of excessive drunkenness, would, as a result, of the mixing of Heavy Water mean death'.'

'Cor lumme!' said Jones.

The conference was breaking up when the A.C. suddenly remembered a minor riddle in the case, but one which clinched an identification.

'Jones,' he said, 'that reminds me. What made you go and look for Peter Greenwell in 'Black' Timmins?'

The fat superintendent, whose fact-finding was regarded as genius in the Yard, but whose complete lack of imagination was a byword and a joke, said:

'Well, A.C., you remember that Rawson said that Greenwell was called by his lady

312

friends a 'courtier', spoke la-di-la and drank pink gins?'

'I remember,' the A.C. agreed.

'So I looked back on all the ladies' men I knew — and I knew a few. And of the lot I could only think of one who spoke la-di-la and drank nothin' but pinks gins. I used me 'Magination.'

A roar of laughter ended the recital.

THE END

We do hope that you have enjoyed reading this large print book.

Did you know that all of our titles are available for purchase?

We publish a wide range of high quality large print books including:
Romances, Mysteries, Classics
General Fiction
Non Fiction and Westerns

Special interest titles available in large print are:
The Little Oxford Dictionary
Music Book, Song Book
Hymn Book, Service Book

Also available from us courtesy of Oxford University Press:
Young Readers' Dictionary
(large print edition)
Young Readers' Thesaurus
(large print edition)

For further information or a free brochure, please contact us at:
Ulverscroft Large Print Books Ltd.,
The Green, Bradgate Road, Anstey,
Leicester, LE7 7FU, England.
Tel: (00 44) **0116 236 4325**
Fax: (00 44) **0116 234 0205**